Praise for *The Tropic of Serpents*

"Smart and nuanced . . . Overwhelmingly fun and a perfectly delightful [summer] read."
—*io9*

★ "Uncompromisingly honest and forthright [and] narrated in Brennan's usual crisp, vivid style."
—*Kirkus*, starred review

Praise for *Voyage of the Basilisk*

"Revelations crash like waves in a satisfying conclusion."
—*Publishers Weekly*

Also by the Author

Doppelganger
Warrior
Witch
Dancing the Warrior
The Doppelganger Omnibus

Onyx Court
Midnight Never Come
In Ashes Lie
A Star Shall Fall
With Fate Conspire Deeds of Men
In London's Shadow: An Onyx Court Omnibus

Wilders
Lies and Prophecy
Chains and Memory

The Memoirs of Lady Trent
A Natural History of Dragons
The Tropic of Serpents
Voyage of the Basilisk
In the Labyrinth of Drakes
Within the Sanctuary of Wings
Turning Darkness into Light

Varekai
Cold-Forged Flame
Lightning in the Blood

Collections
Monstrous Beauty
Maps to Nowhere
Ars Historica
Never After: Thirteen Twists on Familiar Tales

Serials
Born to the Blade, with Michael R. Underwood, Malka Older, and Cassandra Khaw

Non-Fiction
Writing Fight Scenes
Dice Tales: Essays on Roleplaying Games and Storytelling
New Worlds, Year One: A Writer's Guide to the Art of Worldbuilding
New Worlds, Year Two
New Worlds, Year Three

Praise for *Driftwood*

"*Driftwood* is a richly imagined and shifting place. I keep thinking about it weeks after shutting the book. This is what people mean by 'haunting.'"
—Mary Robinette Kowal, author of *The Calculating Stars*

★ "Brennan skillfully builds a multiplicity of worlds, painting each unique and fully developed culture with bold, minimalist strokes and, though readers don't get to spend much time with any single character, rendering each member of the sprawling cast with impressive nuance and subtlety. Exploring found family, adaptation, and hope in the face of apocalypse, Brennan imbues this high-concept fantasy with a strong emotional core. Fantasy fans will be thrilled."
—*Publishers Weekly*, starred review

"Haunting, timeless, and timely. Brennan invented Driftwood, but it feels like she discovered it."
—Max Gladstone author of *The Empress of Forever*

★ "A diverse cast of characters from disparate worlds, each facing their own rapidly approaching mortality, come together to memorialize a missing man—rumored to be immortal—in this new fantasy title from veteran author Brennan . . . Readers will close

the cover aching to read more about Last and his world. An exciting delve into a conglomerate land filled with magic and mystery."
—*Kirkus*, starred review

"Bittersweet and haunting, Brennan's story celebrates the death-defying power of love and everlasting memory."
—Karen Lord, author of *Redemption in Indigo*

Praise for Marie Brennan

"Told in the style of a Victorian memoir, courageous, intelligent and determined Isabella's account is colorful, vigorous and absorbing. A sort of Victorian why-what-whodunit embellished by Brennan's singular upgrade of a fantasy bromide and revitalizingly different viewpoint."
—*Kirkus* on The Memoirs of Lady Trent series

Praise for *A Natural History of Dragons*

★ "Saturated with the joy and urgency of discovery and scientific curiosity."
—*Publishers Weekly*, starred review

DRIFTWOOD

Marie Brennan

Interior and cover design by Elizabeth Story
Author photo by Perry Reichanadter

Tachyon Publications LLC
1459 18th Street #139
San Francisco, CA 94107
415.285.5615
www.tachyonpublications.com
tachyon@tachyonpublications.com

Series Editor: Jacob Weisman
Project Editor: Jaymee Goh

Print ISBN 13: 978-1-61696-346-0
Digital ISBN: 978-1-61696-347-7

Printed in the United States by Versa Press, Inc.

First Edition: 2020
9 7 8 6 5 4 3 2 1

Some of the individual chapters of *Driftwood* have been previously published as the following: "Driftwood" © 2009 by Marie Brennan. First appeared in *Beneath Ceaseless Skies*, April 2009. | "A Heretic by Degrees" © 2008 by Marie Brennan. First appeared in *Orson Scott Card's Intergalactic Medicine Show*, December 2008. | "Into the Wind" © 2017 by Marie Brennan. First appeared in *Children of a Different Sky*, edited by Alma Alexander (Kos Books). | "The Ascent of Unreason" © 2012 by Marie Brennan. First appeared in *Beneath Ceaseless Skies*, September 2012. | "Remembering Light" © 2010 by Marie Brennan. First appeared in *Beneath Ceaseless Skies*, June 2010. | "Smiling at the End of the World" © by Marie Brennan. First appeared on *Swan Tower: Home of Author Marie Brennan*. | "The God of Driftwood" © 2020 Marie Brennan. Original to this book.

DRIFT WOOD

MARIE BRENNAN

TACHYON · SAN FRANCISCO

Driftwood

IN THE DAYS before their world shattered, crumbled, and finally fetched up against that cluster of old realities known as Driftwood, they were called the Valraisangenek.

One of their scholars once spent a week lecturing me on that name alone, before I was allowed to learn anything else. Valraisangenek: echoing their once-proud world of Valrassuith, "The Perfect Circle"—itself based on the ancient root word of *velar*, "totality"—and their race's legendary founder Saneig, "Chosen of San," chosen of the Supreme Goddess, from whom they were all descended (*genkoi*). A name full of meaning, for those who know how to read it. But most people think the name of the Valraisangenek is too long and difficult to be worth remembering, especially when there are so few of them left. These days, everyone just calls them the Greens.

After all, that name has the advantage of being so obvious anybody could remember it—or at least attach it to the appropriate target on sight. Somebody walks in with hair like sea foam, eyes like emeralds, and skin like moss? You're looking at a Green. Slap on whatever the word is for "green" in your language, and you're set to go. Or "blue/green," if your people don't distinguish those two colors, or "red/green" if your race is color-blind, although in that latter case you might run a risk of confusing a Green with a Kakt. But the red-skinned Kakts are numerous enough, and well-known enough, not to mention horned enough, that if you're not smart enough to tell them apart from the Greens, you won't last long in Driftwood anyway.

The Kakts' world is so newly Drifted that on three sides it still borders on nothing but Mist. The calendarists I know figure within a year it'll share a boundary with Egnuren—a Kakt year, that is; nearly two Egnuren years—but I don't recommend telling the Kakts that. Most of them still deny the Driftwood thing. They're new; they're proud. They don't want to admit that their world is gone, and they're all that's left of it.

The Greens know better. Hard to deny the death

of your world when it's shrunk down to a small ghetto whose name hardly anybody bothers to remember. There are theories on how to slow the decay, of course, and back in the day the Greens tried them all. Stay home and pretend Driftwood isn't there. Speak only your own language. Breed only with your own kind. And pray, pray, pray to your gods, as if Driftwood is some kind of test they're putting you through, or a bad dream you can wake up from.

None of it helps. I should know.

But no one listens when I tell them.

Alsanit found him in a Drifter bar. Had her mission been any less urgent, she would not have gone; she was pure Valraisangenek—a "one-blood," in Driftwood parlance—and among the Drifters with their mixed ancestry she stuck out like an emerald in sand. But the Circle had wasted too much time already in doubt; once the decision was made, she left within the day. The whispers and stares of foreigners were nothing, the contempt and even the risk of being mugged, when weighed against her people's need.

The bar was called Spit in the Crush's Eye, and it lay nearly across the Shreds from what was left of Valrassuith. Greenhole, to its neighbors, and even most of the Valrai called it that, these days. That was why Alsanit was braving the stares of the Drifters. Two days ago, *she* had called her home Greenhole.

If something didn't change, they were doomed.

She went from Greenhole to Wash to Heppa to Hotside, and then after that she was into Shreds she didn't know. She got snowed on in the place after Hotside, and two Shreds after that got chased by things that looked like dogs but weren't, but the directions she'd gotten were good, and after about four hours of walking she found herself on the border between Chopper and Tatu, at Spit in the Crush's Eye.

The bar suited its name, being defiantly cobbled together from fragments of a dozen worlds, patched with reed bundles, sheets of scrap metal, even what looked like half the trunk of a tree. Alsanit received the expected stares and mutters when she walked through the door, but this was far from Valras-suith, far from where her people were known; they were reacting to her as a one-blood, a non-Drifter, not as a Green. She wasn't the only one-blood in the bar, though, for at the far wall, she saw the man she sought.

He was tall enough to draw the eye even when sitting; that was how Alsanit first spotted him. Drifters, crossbreeds that they were, tended to average out the range of heights found among Driftwood's races. And even in the murky light of the bar, his skin shimmered a silvery blue, undulled by any foreign pigmentation, against which his black hair made a sharp contrast. But the sight of a fellow one-blood did not reassure Alsanit. There was a certain uniformity to the unpredictability of Drifters. One-bloods had their own ways, and she did not know what this man's ways were.

Walking over to him took much of her courage.

"Are you Last?" she asked, in one of the more widely used pidgin dialects of her side of the Shreds.

"I am," he said easily, in the same dialect. "You?"

"Alsanit."

His teeth glinted pure silver when he smiled. "I'm honored, then."

Alsanit blinked. "Honored?"

"Your name. 'Sworn to San'? No, 'Faithful to.' You're one of the Valrai. High-ranking. Only your important women have San's name in their own."

Alsanit wondered if her jaw was on the floor. Valrai. Not "Greens." And he *knew* them, knew their ways. They were in a bar clear across the Shreds from Valrassuith, and he knew what her name meant. Even the people of the neighboring Shreds didn't bother with that.

Last's smile widened into a grin. "Come on—you came looking for me; didn't you know what to expect? I'm a guide. It's my job to know things like that."

With effort, Alsanit regained her composure. "Yes. But I thought I came from outside your usual territory."

"You do. But it happens I used to have a lover who was Valrai. I still remember some things."

Alsanit wondered who the lover had been. If the stories were true, then odds were good the woman or man was long dead. She decided not to ask, though whether it was because she feared she wouldn't know the person, or because she feared she *would*, she could not have said.

Last leaned back in his chair and interlaced his long fingers. The nails gleamed dark—natural color, or some kind of lacquer? Meaning could be hidden in the smallest of details; for all she knew, among his people, dark nails were the mark of an assassin, or a slave, or nothing whatsoever. All she could do was try to ride the waves of interaction as they rose and fell.

She thought of the stories her people's priests still told—about waves, about the sea—and swallowed tears. The sea was ages gone.

"Let's get to business," Last said. "What is it you need? Interpreter? Somebody to tell you the ways of another Shred? Business contacts?"

"Answers," Alsanit said, raising her chin and meeting his deep black eyes. "*An* answer. To the only question worth asking in this place."

He did not move, but the life drained out of his face, leaving his expression mask-like. Finally he clicked his tongue sharply, a Shreds mannerism that meant absolute negation. "Wrong person, Green."

The name hurt, but she didn't let it show. She clicked back at him, adopting his own slang. "You answered to the name. You fit the description. I know who you are—*what* you are—and I *need* that answer."

Last stood, abruptly, his thighs hitting the table and scraping it sharply across the floor. Conversation in the bar stuttered to a halt as heads turned to look.

"*Wrong person,*" he repeated, his voice carrying to the far corners of the room. "I have no answers. Sorry you came all this way for nothing."

His long legs carried him quickly out of the bar. Alsanit leapt to her feet, intending to pursue, but found her way blocked by a pair of Drifters almost as wide as they were tall, who either didn't understand any of the pidgins she spoke or were pretending not to. They advanced on her until she found herself backed up to a door on the other side of the room, and then they stood there until she gave up and left. Outside, in the streets of Chopper, she tried to find Last—but he had vanished.

Life is different in the Shreds. Out on the very edges of Driftwood, places like Kakt, a determined person can live her whole life pretending her home is still its own world. A little farther in, when things have gotten smaller and you're not by the Mist anymore, you start thinking of your world as a country; you learn about your neighbors, trade with them, set up embassies in their territory. But in the Shreds, there's no ignoring the weirdnesses of Driftwood, the way it's summer on one street and winter on another, day here and night there, obedient to your laws of reality in your own ghetto, but operating by a totally different set of rules three houses down.

Don't ask how it works. It's Driftwood. Patchwork of world fragments, illogic made concrete. It just *is*, and you learn to live with it.

And if you learn to live with it well enough, you can even make some money at it. Pack as many languages into your head as you can, figure out the rules at work in some given set of ghettos, and set up shop as a tour guide. Or something like that. I hate giving tours to Edgers, when they come into the Shreds for kicks. Not because I'm bitter—I got over hating Edgers for their big, solid realities long ago— but because they're oblivious. They don't get how the Shreds work, and they don't want to.

I'm here for the Shredders, for people whose business takes them out of familiar territory, and who want—or need—to learn the ropes where they're going. Vigilantes, crosser-merchants, scholars who have abandoned the decay of their own worlds in favor of trying to figure out how it *all* works. They pay me in the coin of their own realms, if there's any left, or in gems, valuable items, even food. How is it that ivnyils only come from the Rooters' reality, but practically everybody has emeralds? How come most food—but not all—is edible for all races? Why are some things so similar, when others are wildly different? Those are the kinds of questions my scholarly clients want to answer. Me, I don't bother. It's enough that Driftwood exists, and I exist within it—still, even after all these years.

Every so often, though, somebody decides I must have the answers. It's hard to be truly famous in Driftwood; at the Edge, people don't talk much about stuff outside their own reality, and in the Shreds, stories get stopped by language barriers every few blocks. To really become famous, you have to be around for a long time, and then you run into the problem that, oops, you and your reality have been pushed right to the Crush, and you've faded out of existence entirely, along with everybody who knew you.

Pretty much the only way to be famous throughout Driftwood is to still be here, long after the Crush should have gotten you.

Most people figure it's just a story. Sure, I've been around so long even your granny thinks I'm old, but with the way time varies between realities, and the differences in lifespans—the Gnevg live for barely ten of their own short years, the Ost for hundreds—really, there's got to be a way to explain it. And if you're not sure what reality I come from, well, *somebody* has to know, right?

Only a few people chase the stories far enough

to notice this hypothetical "somebody" doesn't seem to exist. People can tell you where I live, or where I spend my time, or how to find me, but they can't tell you where I *come* from.

And of those few people who chase the stories far enough, a very few make the leap of faith to *believing* the stories.

Those are the ones who come and find me, not to hire me as a guide, but to ask me questions.

A question, really. They all ask the same one.

Alsanit hadn't come across the Shreds to hire a guide, but she ended up doing so anyway. She was too far out of familiar neighborhoods; there were too many language and cultural obstacles in her way for her to search without help. So she hired someone, a Drifter, paying him in the seashells the Valrai used as currency, which had merit in some Shreds as medicine, though not for the Valrai themselves. She sent a messenger back home to explain her continued absence, then grimly settled into the task of running Last to ground.

It was a dangerous proposition. She had no way of knowing whether the people she hired or spoke to were trustworthy; it was safest to assume they weren't. But Alsanit didn't have to return home and speak to the Circle to know what they would tell her.

If she failed in this mission, her life was meaningless anyway, along with that of every last Valrai. So what did it matter, that she was risking it here?

Her guide turned out to be reliable, even if several of the informants they approached tried to kill them. Alsanit lost track of how much time they spent searching; away from Valrassuith, she found it hard to maintain familiar standards of time, and days and nights were of different lengths in every Shred she went through. Instead, she kept track of how many shells she had left, and worried over how quickly she was spending them. Before much longer, she would have to return home for more—and she had no idea how much Last would charge for his answer, should she persuade him to give it. Maybe more than all of her people had to give.

But they would find a way to pay.

When Alsanit's shells were nearly gone, her guide found him.

The guide's final service for Alsanit involved kicking in Last's door. Then he was gone down the stairs, off to enjoy the wealth he'd earned, leaving Alsanit standing in Last's doorway with Last's knife at her throat.

"I've killed people for less than this," he told her, calmly, as if the information were no more significant than directions to the nearest Shred boundary.

"Kill me, then," Alsanit said. "It doesn't matter. I'm dead anyway. *All* of my people are."

"Everyone's dead," Last said. "That's Driftwood. In the end, every person, every street, every world will fade and crumble and die."

"Except you."

"Verdict's still out. Who says I won't die someday, like everyone else?"

"You've lasted longer than everyone else. You've cheated Driftwood so far. And I need to know how."

For a moment he stood there, knife pressed against the fragile skin of her throat, and Alsanit truly didn't know whether he would do it or not. "It might be a mercy, killing you," he whispered, as if talking to himself.

The sure knowledge that her world would die without his help gave Alsanit a simultaneous serenity and recklessness that made her words much more than mere bluff. "So do it."

The knife pressed more sharply.

"Or answer my question."

Last's hand trembled.

"Save my world," Alsanit said, "or kill me now."

He did neither. He grabbed her by the shoulder, shoved her to the floor, and left. Alsanit should have chased him, but her legs were too limp. She sat on the tiled floor of the room he rented in a Shred whose name she had already forgotten, shaking and on the edge of tears, and knew her people were doomed.

There are a lot of crackpot theories out there about me. One of my favorites, in a black-humor kind of way, is that my world was the first one, the original core the rest of Driftwood drifted up against. A special variant on that theory says I was the first being of that reality, formed by the local gods out of clay or corn or wood or shit or whatever, that I've been here since the beginning, and will be here until the end.

It used to embarrass me, that people said that kind of thing. It makes me into a god, and I'm not; I hate it when people treat me like one. But after a while, the embarrassment wears off, and you learn to deal. It's a creative idea, at least, better than some I've heard. But no—my world wasn't the first one, and I'm not the first man.

Even the people who don't buy into that notion tend to treat me with a reverence that makes me uncomfortable. I'd rather live my life as a guide, teaching people how to make their way across the wilderness of the Shreds, until the Shreds I know shrink down and slip into the Crush and I have to learn some new ones. I've gotten over mourning the loss of those worlds. They all die, in the end, so you might as well get over it. Sometimes I get hired by scholars who want to know about realities that are long gone, and then I get melancholy, remembering songs no one sings anymore, friends and lovers dead for ages, restaurants I'll never eat at again. My memory goes back a long way: the only immortality any of these places get.

But I don't remember how Driftwood began. I'm not *that* old. For all I know, it's gone on forever, and never had a beginning; maybe there have always been worlds out there, having apocalypses and falling apart and eventually fetching up against the ever-shifting face of Driftwood. Maybe Driftwood is an agreement among the gods, a final mercy, giving their worlds a chance to come to terms with death before it finishes happening.

Or maybe Driftwood is their joke on us.

Part of me hopes so, and hopes that the gods are getting a good laugh out of it. Nobody else is.

She stayed in Last's rented room, first sitting numbly on the tiled floor, later curling up and going to sleep. When she woke, she looked around and wondered if there was any point in staying. He had possessions here, yes, but a man who had outlived the death of countless worlds probably did not attach much importance to mere objects. There was no reason to believe he would return.

But if there was no point in staying, neither was there much point in moving. What would she do?

Go home? She could get more seashells, start another search, maybe find Last again. But he would not give her the answer. So she might as well go home and admit defeat to her people.

And then wait for Valrassuith to finish dying.

She would probably die before her world did. They had perhaps another two generations left— maybe more, maybe less; no one knew what hastened or slowed the inevitable decay.

Except Last.

If that was all that going home held for her, then Alsanit might as well stay here and die. It would hurt less than facing her people with her failure.

Night came and went; it seemed longer than night in Valrassuith, but perhaps despair lengthened it. Alsanit sat with her back to a bedpost of carved bone, stared at the wall, and wondered what she should do with herself. Commit suicide? Starve to death? Set up a new life, exiled from her own world? The question filled her with such apathy that when Last reappeared in the doorway, she simply stared at him, dully, half-believing him a figment of her imagination.

He looked down at her for a long moment. The morning light coming in through the room's one small window made him shine slightly, like a god.

"I make no promises," he finally said, in a quiet, heavy voice. "Other people have tried this, and it didn't work for them. They must have done something wrong. But it's the best I can give you."

"I don't ask for promises," Alsanit whispered. "Just for hope."

He nodded, slowly. "Very well. Lots of people try to stay in their own realities, and never go anywhere else. Doesn't save them. But you can't abandon your own world, either; it needs you to survive. So you have to compromise."

Alsanit waited, the words burning themselves into her memory, blazing with the possibility of survival.

"Have someone—your own shoemakers, if you still have any—make boots with hollow spaces in the heels. Take soil, or small stones, from Valrassuith, and put this into the spaces. Wear the boots at all times. If you do that, you bring your own world with you, wherever you go. You'll always be standing on the ground of Valrassuith, no matter where you are. And this may—*may*—save you."

Hope gave Alsanit new life; she roused from her stupor and began to crawl across the floor to where Last stood. Tears of gratitude fell from her eyes.

Last stepped back before she could kiss his feet. "Don't. Please. Just go back to your people."

"I will," Alsanit whispered. "And—thank you. Words are not enough, but . . . *thank you*."

And carrying his words like the treasure they were, she went to give her people hope.

The night after I saw Alsanit for the last time, I drank myself into a stupor. If you want to solve problems, that's a shitty way to do it, but if you want to wallow in your misery, drinking's the way to go. My problem had no solution. All I could do was wallow.

Alsanit wasn't the first to ask me that question, nor the last. I've sworn to myself time and time again that I won't answer when they ask, that I'll just leave, hide, stay away from them. And I try. But they always hunt me down. What else can they do? I'm their one chance at salvation, their final hope for saving their dying worlds. They can't leave until they get their answer.

So I give it to them.

No one ever wants to hear the truth. I've tried telling them, and they refuse to accept it. They prefer lies. So I tell them what they want to hear. I make up some interesting falsehood, something that sounds plausible; maybe I take it from the rantings of a street-side preacher who died four hundred years ago, and to them it sounds new. And they smile, and weep, and thank me; sometimes, like Alsanit, they try to kiss my feet.

And then they go away, and their worlds die.

The lie I gave Alsanit is a special one. It's one I actually tried, along with all the people of my world, back when there *were* such people, back when there was a world I called my own. We put stones in our boot-heels and prayed it would make us safe.

It didn't save them. And it didn't save me. I kept those stones in my boots for seventy-five years after the rest of them were gone, thinking they were the only things keeping me in existence, until the day I got mugged in Ettolch and the mugger stole my boots. Then there was nothing keeping me "grounded," keeping me on my native soil, and still I didn't die, didn't fade, didn't vanish.

I don't know why.

That's the truth no one wants to hear. I don't have the first clue why I'm still around. I've outlived the normal lifespan of my race many times over; even if my world hadn't gone away, I should be dead. I tried all the theories that were in fashion back then, but so did everyone else around me. They're gone, and I'm not. Maybe the answer lies in some subtle interaction of the things I tried; maybe you need to spend precisely this amount of time in your own reality and that amount of time outside of it, while simultaneously eating specific food in specific weights, and if you get the numbers exactly right, behold, immortality.

I doubt it. But then again, what do I know?

Not much. Except that I'm still here, unlike everybody else.

A Note to the Reader

THE PROVENANCE and authenticity of the following collection of texts is, to put it mildly, quite dubious.

The tradition of recording certain kinds of tales is well established in Driftwood, but the ones gathered here go beyond mere recording. They do not follow the forms characteristic of oral storytelling in any world, and unless the scribe credited with writing them down was possessed of telepathic abilities that transcend time, he could not be privy to the thoughts and feelings of the people as described. If he *were* possessed of such abilities, then we might chide him for omitting a great many details we would have liked to see kept for posterity, such as the acclamation of the first Heretic King. Despite these well-founded reservations, however, the tales themselves are seen as having value, and therefore regardless of their historicity, they are worth preserving—as much as anything in Driftwood can be preserved.

If that is damning with faint praise, then the material between the tales merits no such courtesy. We quite simply have no idea where it came from. In the sole manuscript from which this is reproduced, the handwriting is notably different, and none of the explanations for its authorship are convincing. The most persuasive interpretation is that it is purely fictional, invented by some Driftwood tale-teller to provide context for the more authentic narratives it frames. There is no support for the religious interpretation that it is a work of divine authorship, but that theory persists nevertheless.

Such concerns notwithstanding, I pray to the voices of my ancestors and my descendants that readers will find entertainment, comfort, or worthy moral lessons within these pages. For it is only through the telling of our tales that we have hope of immortality.

Jehiwwim iv le qu Cehlor
Scholar of the Reborn College

The Storyteller

N O ONE KNOWS how it starts, because no one is there to see.

The amphitheater has been abandoned for ages, and for good reason. Any living creature that remains within its truncated bowl when that world's sun rises dies . . . or disappears and is never seen again, which amounts to the same thing. As a result, it is that rarest of commodities within the Shreds: a piece of uninhabited dry land.

Not unused, though. The timeworn sandstone benches are solid enough, if not precisely comfortable, and now that someone has knocked down the creepy, insectile statues that used to stand in watch—or possibly in threat—at the top of the stands, the amphitheater is a nice enough place for all kinds of uses, from performances to markets to punishment for the remaining one-bloods of Skyless. They permit others to use the space as they please, but personally consider its open-air nature to be the next worst thing to hell.

Only at night, though. Throughout the day, and for a generous margin before sunrise and after sunset, the amphitheater tends to be deserted. With the differences in cycles between worlds, nobody quite wants to risk guessing wrong about what time it is—nor do they want to experiment and find out just how long the dangerous period is. And since these days only one tunnel leads from Skyless onto the amphitheater floor, and the people of Soggeny and Up-End don't make a habit of climbing the amphitheater's walls, there's not a lot of traffic in or out.

Which means that as near as anyone can tell, the wreath of flowers simply appears, laid there by some unknown hand, their unfading sapphire petals shining with a faint light of their own in the darkness.

It could be for some other purpose. But the sapphire flowers with their ruby stamens come from Aic, growing like hair from the heads of the few remaining Ta-Aici, and the news—the rumor; the joke; the lie—went around Aic just a little while before. So somebody, it seems, has made an assumption.

More than one somebody. The next night, which is supposed to be a market night, the wreath has company: a tiny stone pyramid, three candles, a shoe, a blunted knife, six torn pieces of fabric. The meaning of the things left there varies, and sometimes they don't have any beyond the personal, but the ripped cloth is clear.

In the Shreds of Driftwood, that is a sign of mourning.

After that, everybody sees the pile grow. The market goes on as it should, but other people come, too: Drifters and one-bloods alike, from farther Shreds like Pool, from the nearer parts of the Ring, even an Edger or two who happens to be close by. Some come to lay their own tokens on the floor of the amphitheater. Others come just to watch the spectacle, to murmur questions and doubts at each other.

Is it true?

The whole thing is a joke.

I don't believe it anyway. Never have. This is Driftwood; we all know how it works.

How can anybody be sure?

Febrenew is there before the second night ends. He keeps the latest iteration of a long series of bars called Spit in the Crush's Eye—or rather, kept. It most recently conducted its business in an improbable cavern, carved out of solid rock beneath a stretch of viscous mud that sucks in anyone who sets foot on it. The entrances lay through the safer terrain of Nidroef and Whitewall, burrowed underground and propped up with enormous rib bones pillaged from some creature that didn't need them anymore.

But probability has caught up with that cavern,

flooding it with mud, and flooding Febrenew out. He hasn't yet found a new home for the bar, and while the amphitheater certainly isn't a candidate, it will do as a temporary source of profit. With so many people gathering, some of them are bound to want food and drink.

Answers, too—but unlike some of his predecessors, Febrenew is scrupulous about his gossip. When a woman asks him if he knows anything, he tells her the truth, which is that he knows no more than anyone else. But it doesn't stop her from loitering nearby, then making periodic arcs through the amphitheater, questioning other onlookers. She's a one-blood, her skin as dark as rich soil, hair coiled against her scalp in intricate gold-threaded knots. The sort of style people only bother with when there's still meaning behind it. An exile from her own world, maybe; there are enough of them around.

And even Febrenew doesn't know everyone. The Drifter community is too complicated for that, held together by its differences as much as anything else. He doesn't know that woman, or the silent old man who takes up station at the top of the benches and sits there eating seeds, or the small, lizard-like creature that conveys through mime that it will conjure water to wash cups for him in exchange for some beer.

Nor does he know the man who approaches the

growing mound of trinkets not long after the sun sets on the third night, bearing an ancient mask in his hands.

Others in the amphitheater are familiar with him: Eshap, one of many who hires himself out as a laborer in the fields of I Grun I, which has land but very few survivors, and those few well-enough armed to prevent a wholesale takeover of their world. He has the medium brown skin and medium brown hair that tend to be the result of averaging out a dozen different races, but a few touches—scalloped ears; four fingers on each hand—that show an ancestor or two peeking through. Driftwood encompasses every kind of creature at one time or another, but certain traits are more common than others.

No one there has seen the mask before.

It is carved out of wood and still carries traces of paint in the hollows of its contours, though most of the pigment has worn away. Unlike the abstracted or exaggerated style of many masks, this one has been carved to look as lifelike as possible—almost a portrait, rendered in wood. A portrait of a man's face, with a high forehead and a full-lipped mouth.

Those nearest enough to Eshap, comparing his features to the ones he holds, can see the faintest hint of resemblance. One of the observers, Lazr-iminya, has enough Sednibamri ancestry to be exceptionally long-lived; she remembers when there were still people in whom those features were common.

Eshap doesn't lay the mask on the pile. Instead he turns to face the seats of the amphitheater, salted with a few score observers, doubters, and mourners, and speaks.

"My great-grandmother's people are gone now," he says in one of the better-known pidgins, the ephemeral bridges that link the Drifter community together. "She was the last who claimed them as her own—though truth be told, even she was more Drifter than anything else. But she held on to the name anyway. And to this mask. And to the story of why she kept it, long after it stopped meaning anything to anybody but her."

The murmurs die away. Some people watch him with a cynical eye, but no one interrupts, or leaves.

Eshap's voice grows stronger as he goes on. The back wall of the amphitheater throws the sound forward, reaching the highest seats. "I don't count myself as Miqerin, not like she did . . . but the mask is mine. And the story. And if there's one thing Driftwood can't take from us, it's stories. As long as we tell them, and go on telling them, they live. Even if—"

His voice breaks, and his chin dips. A few people mutter; one, apparently bored with the spectacle, turns and heads for the single tunnel that still gives access to the amphitheater's floor.

But old Lazr-iminya is a grandmother to half the Shreds, and Eshap is no exception. She creaks forward and lays one hand on his wrist, her fingers wrinkled and knobby and strong. "Tell the story, son," she says.

Eshap draws in a deep breath, tucks the mask face-in against his chest, and begins.

A Heretic by Degrees

THE KING WAS DYING, and nothing in the world could save him.

The Councillor Paramount said, "Then we must look outside the world for help."

The suggestion was heretical, and treasonous to boot. Two years before, the king had established by sacred decree that there was only one world, and that nothing lay beyond its bounds; anything seen there was a delusion, a final torment sent to test the faithful before their eventual salvation. And for two years, his councillors and subjects had respected his word.

Now they faced a choice. Disobey the king—or lose him. Commit treason, or let him die, and with him, the last remnant of the sacred royal line.

The Councillor Paramount's statement met with a lengthy, embarrassed, indecisive silence.

By the standards of his predecessors, Qoress was new to the position of Councillor Paramount; he had been in service for a mere two years. The man who served before him had gone into the spaces outside the world, and only his right arm and half of his head had come back. Thus the decree, and thus the need for a new Councillor Paramount.

One might expect from this that Qoress would be the last man to suggest that something might exist outside the world, much less that help might exist in those places. But he was a thoughtful man, and moreover one who cared for his king; also, he knew that his fellow councillors were a weak-willed lot who would consider and discuss and debate and do everything in their power to avoid making a decision, for whoever brought matters to such a point could subsequently be blamed for it.

From out of the rustling of ceremonial robes and uncomfortable creaking of stools came one timid, anonymous voice. "But—we wouldn't know where to *start.*"

Their lack of spine served Qoress' purpose, for it meant they wouldn't argue with him. He smiled down at them all, hands arranged in the gesture of Serene Confidence. "Do you really believe all of His Holiness' subjects have obeyed that decree?"

The councillors would have gone traipsing about the capital in a vermilion-robed herd, looking for criminals who had gone outside the world, had Qoress not stopped them. They'd been chosen based on lineal tradition and priestly oracular signs, not espionage capabilities. No one outside the palace knew the king was dying, and Qoress wanted to keep it that way.

Finding the help they needed took money they did not have, and time, which was even more precious. But their investment was finally rewarded when the Holy Royal Guard brought a man to Qoress' chambers, on the right sort of charge of treason and heresy.

"You got no proof," were the first words out of the man's mouth when the guards shoved him to his knees.

Qoress regarded the man for a careful moment. His stocky shoulders and barrel chest made him appear nearly as wide as he was tall; too much of one dimension, and not enough of the other. By the ancient principles of harmonious bodily proportion that governed palace life, the man was entirely displeasing, and moreover the length of his nose indicated an untrustworthy nature. But the palace inhabitants, harmonious of build though they might be, did not have the expertise he needed.

Qoress indicated with a flick of his fingers that the guards should leave.

When the two of them were alone in the room,

he said, "You have been brought here for a purpose. I swear beneath the foot of the Agate God that if you help us, your crimes will be forgiven, in the eyes of both gods and men."

The man's dull face lit up slowly at his words.

"*But*," Qoress added, before the man could speak, "this matter is one of utmost security. Therefore, I also swear beneath the foot of the Agate God that if you betray even the tiniest part of this matter to anyone in the world, your blood will boil in your veins, your eyes will roast in their sockets, and your skin will crisp from your flesh, your flesh from your bones, until nothing remains of you but a pile of ash, soon scattered by the wind. Do you understand me?"

After a frozen moment of horror, the man swallowed convulsively and nodded.

"Very well," Qoress said. His own words left a bitter taste in his mouth. Not because he regretted the necessity of threats; he would burn a hundred men to ash if it would save the king. No, the bitterness came because it would *not* save the king. He could kill, but he could not heal.

He had to hope that someone else could.

Qoress stood before the man, clasping his hands in the gesture of Sorrowful Resolution. "You have been outside the world," he said. "We have need of your experience. It is said that many wonders exist in the places we do not speak of. Is an ability to heal the sick and dying among those wonders?"

It was remarkable, Qoress reflected some time later, how quickly one adjusted to strangeness when there was need. Since becoming Councillor Paramount, he had not once been within three paces of anyone so common and vulgar as Heint, the criminal he had recruited, but now they stood side by side at a map table, studying the image and speaking heresy.

Heint's blunt finger stabbed down at a town. "That ain't there anymore. Nor that. Nor that. And the river's dried up, with the spring gone." With one swoop, his unmanicured nail denied the existence of an entire swath of the world.

Worse than Qoress had realized, then. There had been a second decree, not long after his ascension to Paramountcy, declaring that all of the towns, rivers, fields, and other portions of the world were where they had always been. Obedient to the king's sacred word, everyone had disregarded the lack of communication with a number of towns in the east, the disappearance of those who had lived there. But what Heint was describing went well beyond the vanished area Qoress knew had provoked the decree.

So the rumors were true. The world—what remained of it after the judgment of the gods had begun—was continuing to fade.

But that was not Qoress' true concern. "Beyond that?"

"Beyond that," Heint said, "there are two places.

Up here—" He tapped the northern edge of the disputed area. "You don't want to go there. Creatures there look like six-armed wolves, eat anybody who comes near them. That's what happened to the guy before you. Lucky for us they don't much want to leave their home. But to the southeast . . . there, we might have luck."

Qoress stared at the southern portion of the map, the lines and letters melting away in his mind as the places they marked had melted, leaving a blank, unknown space. "What lies to the southeast?"

Heint grinned at him, showing crooked teeth. "Another world."

The arms of the chair were tangling the sleeves of even the relatively plain robes Qoress had worn to the meeting, and the seat was too high for him to sit comfortably. He was already vexed by his inability to understand the choppy clicks that passed for language in this place; little things like awkward furniture frayed his temper still further. But he could not trust Heint to handle this without supervision, and so here he was, committing an unthinkable crime: not just speaking of a place his king had told him didn't exist, but going there in person.

He had seen a disturbing number of his countrymen walking the tunnels that passed for streets in this . . . he was not yet comfortable with terming it a world. Yet he did not know what else to call the place; it wasn't a delusion, whatever the king's decree had said. He knew it the minute he stepped over the border and found himself beneath a punishing trio of suns that made the need for underground dwelling immediately apparent. And that was *before* he met any of the impossibly slender people who inhabited it, as unlike the stocky bodies of Qoress' people as dandelion fluff was to a log.

Heint appeared to be arguing with his interlocutor, though given the sharp edges of the language, it was hard to tell disagreement from friendly speech. Certainly there was much back-and-forth, with hand-waving on Heint's part, and rippling shrugs that Qoress thought might be the equivalent on the other fellow's part.

Finally Heint turned to Qoress and sighed. "Right. It's going to be more complicated than that."

The words produced a peculiar mixture of hope and dread in Qoress' heart. "What do you mean?"

"They can't heal anybody," Heint said. "In fact, they don't *believe* in healing anybody; if you get sick or hurt, then you've offended . . . spit me, I don't even know what he said you've offended. Some kind of god, I guess. And he says none of the worlds they border on can do anything more than medicine—only he calls it 'blasphemy juice,' which is pretty funny, I thought." He caught Qoress' expression and hurried onward. "But that doesn't mean we're at a wall.

"See, it goes way past here, right? There's our world, and there's this place, and the place with the wolf-things north of here—only I guess it's west for them; it's where their suns set, anyway—I don't know, I'm still not great with their language. But they've got other worlds on their borders, and *those* places border other places *too*."

Despite his resolution to do whatever he must to save the king, Qoress was deeply uncomfortable with this kind of talk. "Please come to your point, if you have one."

Heint took a deep breath. "My point is, they say there's a guy who can help. Not by healing, but by taking us to somebody who can. He's a guide. Knows a bunch of different worlds. If there's any place where somebody can wave their hands and make a dying man get well, he'll know where to find it. And he'll take you there and back. For a price."

Already this had gone well beyond what Qoress had in mind when he first suggested looking outside the world for help. But could he turn back now? Salvation for the king might lie just a few steps farther over the edge.

"Find me this man," he said.

The man insisted, via intermediaries, on meeting them somewhere else.

Heint went with Qoress, but he no longer led the way; his heretical crimes had only extended to the tunnel-place and one trip, brief and ill-advised, to the place of the wolf-people. They had a new guide for this journey, a man of the tunnel-place who knew the realms beyond.

Together the three of them sailed, with guards, across a small and inexplicable stretch of sea, whose sky of shifting colors marked it as yet another place—another world, though Qoress' mind still shied from the term. The guards were there to stab over the boat's edges at things beneath the water's surface which Qoress chose not to examine too closely.

The place beyond that seemed sane by contrast. The people were taller and slimmer than Qoress' own, but not too strange, and the sky had the proper pair of suns, not too bright.

The man they met there was quite different.

His hair was black like theirs, but he stood a head taller than the people of that place, with skin silvery blue next to their cinnamon. Standing in an open-air pavilion with the willowy dandelion-fluff of their guide and guards, surrounded by cinnamon-skinned locals, with Heint almost strange in his familiarity, Qoress felt disorientation as sharp as pain. He buried his hands in his sleeves—the gesture of Reserved

Wisdom, not that he felt particularly reserved or wise, not that these people could recognize it—and tipped his head politely to the man.

One of the locals held out a bowl of pure blue glass to Qoress, and said something to their guide.

The guide translated for Heint, and Heint translated for Qoress. "He wants you to spit in the bowl. Three times."

The request was disgusting, but Qoress supposed it to be some manner of traditional ritual, and possibly an insult if he refused. So he did as he was bid, struggling to muster enough saliva the third time. His mouth was very dry.

The local carried it across to the tall stranger, who likewise spat three times.

Again the bowl to Qoress, and again the chain of translations. Heint said, "Now you drink it."

"I most certainly will *not*," Qoress snapped. His stomach heaved at the thought. "I don't know what quaint local custom this is meant to be, but if they think that I will—"

Long before he got that far in his outraged objection, the stranger was speaking, resulting in a muddled flow as everyone tried to translate for his neighbor and their words swamped Qoress under. Heint had to repeat the message several times before it penetrated. "It'll make things easier—shared speech—oh, just *drink* it, you tight-arsed palace peacock," and thereupon Heint shoved the bowl at

Qoress' lips so he could not help but get some in his mouth, mid-diatribe.

Qoress gagged and jerked back, but by then no one was paying attention to him; the local carried the bowl back to the stranger, who drank the remainder without a qualm.

"There," the stranger said, in perfectly coherent speech. "Unpleasant, I'm afraid, but it's convenient; I'll be sad when this place disappears, and I have to go back to learning languages the hard way."

Qoress' eyes widened against his will; he had been trying very hard not to show surprise at the oddities he encountered. "How—how did you do that?"

"I didn't do it. He did." The stranger pointed at the man with the bowl. "Or the bowl did, maybe—I'm not sure how it works. That's why we met here. Magic often only works in the world it belongs to, but with some things, once they're done, they're done. You and I will be able to communicate no matter where we are. And since you're from the Edge, odds were we would have to go through at least two translators to talk, otherwise."

Traveling through peculiar realms inhabited by people even more peculiar had been enough of a strain on Qoress' mind. This, he felt, was one thing too many. Even though he had come here in search of wonders—in search of a miracle to cure his king—to face, to *taste* evidence of such wonders . . .

Whether he meant to or not, the stranger saved

Qoress from hysterical, disbelieving laughter that would have destroyed his pretense at sanity and control. "Now that we can talk to each other," the guide said, "let's talk fees."

Heint picked up the bag they had brought with them from home. At the heretic's advice, Qoress had gathered samples of many different things, not all of them valuable. As Heint brought the items out, one by one, the stranger studied them with a curious eye. The emerald he set aside with a disinterested shake of his head, but the fire quartz received an approving murmur. He tasted several of the foods, making a face at the lizard-lick, and finally subjected the meshtren in its cage to an extended study.

"All right," he said at last. "What are you hiring me for? I'll guide you there and back by the safest route I know; that's one service. And since you're an Edger, with no languages but your own, I'll serve as translator as well. If you want to bargain with the people we go to, I'll interpret for you, or I can handle it on your behalf. Let me know what you want, and I'll let you know what it'll cost."

None of the other councillors were present for Qoress to consult; he had to make the decision unaided. He scrutinized the man's face, wondering if high cheekbones still signified an adaptable nature when the individual with them was from a different realm entirely, and what the smoothly rounded edges of his ears might mean at all. "I would be obliged if you handled the bargaining," he said at last. No doubt the man would take his own cut of the price, but it was obvious that Qoress did not know what counted as valuable trade-goods. And he would empty the palace treasury to save the king.

The stranger nodded. "All right. For the guide-work and the translation, forty of those stones." He pointed at the fire quartz. "For the healing, I'm going to make some bargains along the way. Bring me three breeding sets of that insect in the cage—pairs or whatever it is they need to reproduce. I know a lady who would be fascinated to have some, and she'll give me shells in trade. Is that acceptable?"

It was acceptable; it was a quivering relief. The meshtren was a pest, nothing more; capturing three breeding trios would be as easy as setting the palace maids to work. It seemed Heint was correct about the odd economics of this place. And forty fire quartzes was a price he would gladly pay.

When Qoress indicated his agreement, the man said something unintelligible to the cinnamon-skinned people standing around, then gestured for Qoress to follow him. "Let's sit down and discuss this, then."

They settled onto long couches in another pavilion, and servants brought bowls of some liquid the stranger advised Qoress and Heint not to drink. "You never know what will poison you," he said. "Not everybody can eat and drink the same things.

I suggest you bring your own food with you when we go."

At last they were relatively alone. The stranger said, "Since we're business partners now, I'll introduce myself. My name is Last. I'm from the Shreds, but I do business near the Edge now and again— guide-work, translation services, and so on. I've got plenty of experience all over Driftwood. Mine are the safest hands you could be in." He paused in his speech and gave Qoress an appraising look. "Does any of that mean a thing to you?"

Qoress wanted to lie; ignorance was a weakness he dared not reveal. His hesitation betrayed him, regardless. "I figured," Last said. "Most Edgers are like that. Let's start with a geography lesson."

He cast about as if looking for something, then caught sight of the carpet. "This will do. It's as close to a useful map of Driftwood as you'll ever get."

The carpet consisted of a set of concentric circles in different shades of blue. Last got up from his seat and crouched at the outermost circle, tapping the pale fibers with one dark-lacquered fingernail. "This is the Edge. Your world is out here. Edge worlds are new to Driftwood. They just had their apocalypses. Outside them is Mist—" He gestured at the floor around the circular rug. "I assume you've got that on at least one side of you, since you can't have been here long.

"Go farther in, you find the Ring." Now his hand

moved inward to a circle of medium blue. "No Mist touching these places, but they're still pretty big. Farther inward of *them*, there's the Shreds." He touched the dark blue circle. "There's no clear boundary between the Ring and the Shreds; depends on how large you think a place has to be to count as a Ring world. The Shreds are the little remnants, neighborhoods and ghettos. And in the center. . . ." A small spot of black lay at the heart of the carpet, and Last looked down at it with an odd expression. "The Crush. Where it all goes to die."

Qoress dodged this stream of heresy rather desperately. "Where are *we* going?"

Last leaned back against his couch with a blithe disregard for propriety. Or perhaps sitting on the floor was acceptable, where he came from. "I know of two places that have healing magic. Well, three, but the Shstri would have you for dinner if we went there, so we won't. One place is about forty-five degrees widdershins of you." He took a small black stone from a pocket in his trousers and laid it out on the edge of the carpet, then set another one much farther inward, on the dark blue, some distance around the circle. "If the first stone's you, the second one is Aalyeng. Our other option is over here." A third stone went on the other side of the black circle from the stone that was Qoress' home.

"What difference is there between them?"

"The people in Aalyeng can cure physical diseases.

In Grai-ni-tar, they can cure pretty much anything—physical, mental, spiritual, whatever."

"And Grai-ni-tar," Qoress said, stumbling over the alien name, "is farther away."

"Yes, but that isn't necessarily a problem. We'd have to go near the Crush, but contrary to popular belief, it can't actually suck you in."

Qoress did not know, and did not want to know, what this Crush was. The nature of the king's ailment was unclear; to be safe, he should go to Grai-ni-tar. But Qoress also did not know how long the king had to live.

"How much," he asked with trepidation, "would it cost to try healing him in both places?"

Last looked mildly surprised at his willingness to spend; not even Heint knew the identity of the sick man, and Qoress was not going to share that information. "Do you still have any mines producing iron ore?" the guide asked, finally. Qoress nodded. "Bring a man's weight in iron ingots, then. People always need raw materials, in the Shreds. We'll go widdershins to Aalyeng, then on to Grai-ni-tar if necessary; it won't be much longer of a trip than if we went to Grai-ni-tar direct. Will that do?"

It would, and Qoress said so, trying to disguise how pathetically grateful he was to have this man's help.

"Fetch your patient, then, and meet me back here," Last said. "Bring the payment, food, and whatever guards you think you need. I'll make our arrangements in the meantime."

Qoress could not pinpoint the moment at which he accepted that the realms they moved through truly were different worlds, but the cause was clear enough. He could not travel across so many of them and not accept it.

It wasn't merely the people—short and tall, slender and fat, pale and dark, sometimes with different numbers of eyes or arms, sometimes nothing like men at all. It wasn't merely the changing number of suns and moons, the abrupt transitions from sweltering heat to icy cold as he stepped over an invisible line in a street. It wasn't merely the architecture, the sounds of the languages, the plants and the animals and the colors of the skies.

Something lay beneath all of these surface changes, however unnerving they might be. Walking from world to world with a troop of guards protecting the palanquin of the dying king, Qoress sensed an irreducible *otherness* every place he went. Some perversion of the natural order brought these places together and made it so he could travel to and within and across them, but it did not make him belong there. He came from another world, and these places were not his.

Last's services, he soon came to recognize, extended beyond merely speaking the necessary languages and knowing the safest path. Whether the guide understood this or not, he aided Qoress by thinking on the councillor's behalf, making pragmatic decisions while Qoress' mind gibbered and twitched under the realization of where he was. Under normal circumstances Qoress would never have conceded such control to another, but he had no choice—a fact never far from his thoughts.

There was no way to track how long they had been traveling, with night and day each seeming to follow the rules of the world they were in, not aligning with each other across boundaries. But they had to stop occasionally to rest, and using that to define a day, they had been traveling for just over a fortnight from the place of the cinnamon-skinned people when Qoress asked Last a question.

He had observed, as they traveled, that the realms they moved through were getting smaller, and now they were nothing more than neighborhoods, areas of a few square blocks that held to a single reality before shifting to another one. They had passed through cities in other worlds, but now it seemed there was nothing but *a* city: a chaotic, unplanned place that would have made the sacred architects scream in despair, a place that made Qoress' mind abandon all hope of finding the order he craved. It was simply easier to let himself float along, surrendering himself to the whirlpool—and that, in turn, brought to mind the blue carpet Last had used as a map, and the things he had said then.

It was evening where they were, though it had been morning in the previous neighborhood; Last had bargained for a large shed they could sleep in for a time. Qoress was inside the shed, because it meant he didn't have to look at all the unfamiliar things outside, but Last was on the front step, watching the city's life go by.

"These places," Qoress said hesitantly to the guide, speaking through the open door. "They are all . . . *worlds.*"

"Yes," Last said. He was filling an oddly-shaped pipe with a scarlet leaf Qoress no longer expected to recognize.

"Worlds which have . . . come to an end."

"They're in the process of it." Instead of lighting the pipe, Last carefully dripped a little bit of water into it, then sucked on the stem with evident pleasure.

Qoress thought of the myriad places they had traveled through, and horror gripped his heart in a fist of iron. "*All* of them?"

Last shrugged. "Every world ends someday. Or maybe I'm wrong; who knows? If a place doesn't come to an end, it doesn't come here. But Driftwood is where worlds come to die."

"Driftwood. That is . . . this place."

"The whole place, from the Crush right out to your home." Last gave him a sidelong look. "People out on the Edge usually deny it; you've got enough of a world left that you can. But it's fading—have you noticed that? Shrinking. Bits just vanish. People die, or vanish with the bits, and though maybe you're still having kids—some worlds do; some don't— your population shrinks with your world. One day there's a place on the other side of you, where before there was only Mist. They've had an apocalypse, too. Different than yours, probably, but the result is the same; there's a fragment that survives, a fragment that isn't done dying, and it came here like all the rest of them. They fade like you do, and as you fade you move inward, because the worlds that lie Crushward of you are doing the same thing. Eventually you're just a little ghetto, hardly anything left. And then you reach the Crush, the heart of Driftwood. The last bits vanish—and then there's nothing."

The utter nihilism of the thought was unendurable. Qoress knew why the center of Driftwood was called the Crush; he felt that force bearing down on him, threatening to undo him entirely.

"Our prophecies," he forced himself to say, "tell us otherwise. Our king will guide us through our tribulations, and lead us to salvation in the paradise of the Agate God. And then will begin the reign of the Amethyst God, and a new birth for the world."

Unimpressed by this information, Last merely

shrugged again. "Could be you're right. I've been around Driftwood for a long time, but I don't claim to be an expert on anybody's gods. There might be another world waiting for you all. But it'll be waiting for you on the other side of the Crush."

They checked the king's health regularly; it wasn't good, but he still lived, and that was reason enough for hope.

But the people of Aalyeng—not people at all, more like serpents with forked and dexterous tails— could not heal the king, and so they moved onward to Grai-ni-tar.

The guards knew who they carried, as did the physician accompanying him. All had been bound to secrecy in the same manner as Heint. The criminal himself was, Qoress hoped, still waiting in the world of the cinnamon-skinned people, to guide them home when they returned. But Qoress wondered how much good that secrecy would do. Fully a score of people had now disobeyed the king's decree, by order of the Councillor Paramount; they had traveled through other worlds and felt the truth of Driftwood for themselves. They were heretics all, now, and what effect would this experience have on them?

Save the king. Nothing else mattered. He would worry about other concerns after the king was well.

And if he was executed for his own crimes, then so be it.

Last guided them through the Shreds in an arc that skirted the Crush. Qoress had no desire to see it with his own eyes. They were attacked by some kind of large bird in one world; the guards' arrows bounced off it, and Last led them at a run over the boundary into the next Shred. Someone killed one of the guards while they were resting, and stole everything off the body, including the clothes, without anyone else hearing. They learned from these lessons and adapted. Qoress, like all councillors, had lived from his birth in the palace, and had been soft and idle to match. Studying the new scars on his forearm, he wondered if his peers on the council would recognize him when he came back.

At last they came to Grai-ni-tar.

The people there, with skin like ink and eyes like stars, did not want anyone to accompany the king's palanquin into the ramshackle building that, even to Qoress' eye, was obviously a makeshift replacement for a temple now lost, decorated with crude approximations of sculptures and murals. Last, seeing Qoress' distress, argued vehemently with the priests. In the end, the two of them were permitted within, while the guards and physician remained outside.

The priests carried the palanquin down a large, dark archway, through a series of three curtains in black, grey, and white, and into a courtyard open to the sky.

There one of their number drew back the palanquin's drapes, murmured over the king, turned to Last, and said a short phrase.

The guide snapped something back, receiving the same phrase in reply, and strode forward to the palanquin himself. Qoress, his stomach in knots, saw the moment Last's shoulders slumped.

"I'm sorry," the guide said, his voice low and defeated. "He's dead."

Qoress woke on a hard, narrow bed, with only one lamp casting a dim light. There was no blessed period of confusion; he knew instantly where he was, and what had happened.

The king was dead.

He rolled over and found himself not alone. Last sat on a low stool nearby, hands working an intricate puzzle of interlocking wooden pieces.

"I'm guessing he was someone important," the guide said softly, not looking at Qoress. "Your king?"

Qoress' words came thickly, from a mouth that no longer saw much point in speaking. "The last of his line." Perhaps this was his punishment for heresy. But why did his world have to be punished alongside him?

"Who was supposed to lead you all to salvation. I remember." Two pieces slid out of the puzzle. Last laid them aside, the dark gloss of his fingernails gleaming in the lamplight. "Can you choose another?"

Qoress' laugh was despairing. "You don't *choose* a king. The gods do. His family was sacred, but they all died when—when the—" His throat closed off. Horror enough, to have lived through the end of the world; he could not tell that tale to this stranger, while lying in a bed worlds away from home.

Last's eyes were still on the puzzle. "Everything comes to an end someday. That's what this place is *for*. But it doesn't make the end hurt any less." The pieces came apart in his hands, without warning, and the puzzle dissolved into disconnected fragments.

Tears blurred Qoress' vision. What would this mean to his people? Suppose this man was right; suppose that Driftwood was the ultimate truth of the end, and that their prophecies of salvation, paradise, and rebirth were a lie. They were still a lie his people could cling to. Without that to hold them together, they had nothing. Anarchy would tear them apart.

"I do have one possibility to offer you." Last's voice stopped the downward spiral of his thoughts.

Sitting up on the edge of the bed, Qoress brushed feebly at his hair, as if his fingers could mend the disarranged braids so easily. There was little hope in his heart, but still he said, "Tell me."

"Two Shreds widdershins of here, there's a place called Rosphe. They can do this trick—it's like a permanent shape-shifting. They can do it to other people. And once it's done, it's done, like the language-magic we performed." Last's long fingers were manipulating the pieces once more. Qoress watched them dance. "None of your people know yet that your king is dead."

The puzzle came back together again, as it had been before, and Qoress realized what Last meant.

He surged to his feet, torn between sickness and murderous fury. "How *dare* you suggest such blasphemy to me? To prey on me when you know I am vulnerable—you calculated every *step* of this conversation, didn't you? Even down to that puzzle, an elegant illustration of your point. I am a heretic and a traitor to my king; I confess this beneath the foot of the Agate God. But even I, fallen man that I am, would not presume to such a masquerade."

Last was undisturbed by his outburst. "It's up to you," he said easily, studying the reconstructed puzzle. "Since there was no healing, the priests here have not taken their fee. You could pay it to the people in Rosphe instead. But if this is your decision, then I'll lead you home, as agreed."

Finally he looked up at Qoress, meeting his eyes for the first time since the councillor awoke. "I take my services very seriously. I'm not just a guide, not just a translator; I help people survive in Driftwood.

As much as I can, against the breakdown that eventually claims it all. So I offer you what help I can. Whether or not you take it is up to you."

He stood and set the puzzle on his vacated stool. "When you're ready to come out, the priests will prepare a bath and food for you. I'll wait in the courtyard. From there, I'll take you wherever you want to go."

Then he departed, leaving Qoress alone with the delicate puzzle of wood.

A wave of noise surged up from the open plaza before the holy palace, as if the crowds assembled there spoke with one roaring voice. Gold and copper, studded with jewels, shone from the platform where the councillors stood in their vermilion robes.

A guard stepped forward and lifted a spear. Spiked on the end of it, brow still bearing the mark of his office, was the head of the former Councillor Paramount. No one knew the specifics of his crime, but his accomplices had been spared; all the guilt lay on Qoress, and he had died a heretic's death.

So it was, by order of the king.

At the border with the tunnel-world, Last hefted his pack onto one shoulder. No one had paid him for this trip out to the Edge; he'd come of his own will, to see what happened.

The man at his side did not wear the heavy, ornate robes of the king. They drew too much attention, and he was not accustomed to them anyway.

"I am damned for this," the king said.

Last shrugged. "Maybe. Maybe not. But you have a chance to help your people, and that's got to count for something. You're the king now: heresy will be what you say it is." He grinned, a brief flash of silver teeth. "Maybe you'll be the last, best heretic."

The jest made Qoress flinch, but Last might be right. He smoothed his expression and gripped Last's hand. "May all the gods smile on your journey."

He stood at the edge of his world and watched until the guide vanished into the tunnels, his own words echoing in his mind. Whether their paradise lay beyond the Crush or not, they could not ignore where they were. At least now his people would face Driftwood with their eyes open, guided by one who, if he did not understand it, was willing to learn.

If heresy could lead to salvation, then he would find a way.

recorded by Yilime

The Defender

THE CLUSTER OF STARS that provides most of the nighttime light sets over the wall the amphitheater shares with Soggeny while Eshap is talking, leaving the place in near-total darkness. But one of the other Drifters who works with him in the fields of I Grun I digs in the pile and comes up with a set of three sticks joined by a ring; when they twist the sticks to form a tripod, a light flares and rises from where the legs of the tripod meet. It bathes the entire amphitheater in gentle amber warmth.

Eshap murmurs his thanks, then holds up the mask. "This was the face of their king—the face Qoress took on, for the sake of his people. My great-grandmother was the last to rule as king; I haven't put it on. There's no point in doing it when there aren't any Miqerni to lead anymore. But I have this mask—my great-grandmother and all the Miqerni before her had it—because of Last. Because he showed Qoress a way to adapt. Without that. . . ." He shook his head. "They fell apart in the end. Lost faith in their kings, the promises of the priests—the usual tale. But it would have happened a lot sooner without his help. I may be a Drifter, not Miqerin, but I'm still grateful to Last for that."

Silence has more or less reigned throughout his story, the assembled Drifters and occasional one-blood respecting Eshap enough to give him a proper hearing. It continues to hold as he reverently lays the mask on the nearest slope of the pile.

Then it is broken by a derisive snort.

The sound comes from Kuondae. Eshap knows her only distantly: a cynical shadow on the edge of his sphere, more inclined to earn her living with her mind than her hands. An interpreter and sometime spy, for those who can tolerate the sharp edge of her tongue. The dark-skinned woman with the gold in her hair spoke to Kuondae just before Eshap's story began, but what Kuondae might have said—and how much truth it held—is anyone's guess.

Because the bitterness in Kuondae runs to the bone. Two of her parents were Drifters, but the third was Yrecir, and chose her pair of mates from outside her own people, in defiance of the Yrecra insistence on breeding only within their own boundaries.

When she found herself regretting that choice, she abandoned her daughter to the Shreds.

Kuondae lacks the full pelt of a proper Yrecir, but her grey-tinged skin is covered in a fine, soft layer of fuzz. It gives her a feline appearance as she perches on the low wall separating the amphitheater seats from the stage.

"Right," she says, in a carrying, contemptuous voice. "Last is such a *generous* man, a positive wellspring of charity. Never ever accepts payment for his help, even when people press it on him . . . oh, sorry. I'm confusing him with a saint. Or a god."

An uncomfortable ripple goes through the amphitheater at that last barb. One quiet figure near the bottom of the stands smiles. He wears a blue-grey robe, and sits with a scrolling lap-desk and pen; he has been here since the second night, making a list of the items added to the pile. And, more recently, recording Eshap's story.

Kuondae hops down from the wall and circles the pile of mementos, like a predator eyeing a carcass. "Last charged my first-father a month's wages to go into Yr-alani and get medicine for me when my fur started to fall out. Generous?" She spits in Eshap's direction. "Not hardly."

Someone behind her says, "He paid most of that *to* the Yrecir, for the medicine."

"So he claimed." Kuondae's lip curls. "But he always keeps some for himself, doesn't he?"

"He still had to eat!" another person shouts from up in the stands.

Kuondae flicks her fingers dismissively in that general direction. "Does he? I thought the man can't die. Every meal he's ever eaten—couldn't that have gone into the mouth of a beggar instead? Some sad little orphan of a dead world?" The bitter acid of her tone mocks the notion. Sometimes the Drifter community takes care of the needy, the abandoned . . . but not always. As Kuondae knows all too well.

She pivots to face Eshap as if to turn her back on that memory. "I heard your story, but I took something different from it. Last is a *liar*. He helped Qoress trick your people, and he did it so well, they decided to cling to that trick like it was a holy writ from the Amber God or whatever rock you said they were worshipping."

Eshap's hands ball into fists. She snatches up a glass bottle and holds it like a knife, grinning. Her teeth are smaller than her mother's, but still sharp. "I bet he's watching this whole thing from nearby, laughing his ass off. When nobody's looking, he'll come take a few choice things from this heap and keep them for himself."

"You're wrong."

If Kuondae resembles a small, furred predator, Ioi might to be trying to mimic a bird. The sides of their head are shaved, and white feathers are braided into the strip of hair that remains, stark against the warm rose-gold of their skin. They hold no gift, but come to join the other two on the stage floor anyway, like a performer making their entrance.

Kuondae's sharp-toothed smile only deepens. "Which part? The lying? The profit? Or . . . the part where he's still alive?"

Another murmur runs through the amphitheater, but Ioi ignores it. "If he were as selfish as you say, then he wouldn't spend someone's entire lifetime helping them."

In Driftwood, a claim like that comes with a fair bit of wiggle room. One of the new worlds on the Edge is inhabited by people that are born and die in less time than it takes most races to gestate, incubate, or otherwise get their offspring ready for life. But such quibbles are the stuff of smart-ass arguments in bars, and Kuondae doesn't take the bait.

She merely waves her hand and returns to her perch on the wall. "So you have a pretty little story of your own. Tell it if you want . . . it will make no difference."

Into the Wind

THE TENEMENTS presented a blank face to the border: an unbroken expanse of wall, windowless, gapless, resolutely blind to the place that used to be Oneua. Only at the edges of the tenements could one pass through, entering the quiet and sunlit strip of weeds that separated the buildings from the world their inhabitants had once called home.

Eyo stood in the weeds, an arm's length from the border. The howling sands formed a wall in front of her, close enough to touch. They clouded the light of Oneua's suns, until she could barely make out the nearest structure, the smooth lines of its walls eroded and broken by the incessant rasp of the sands. And yet where she stood, with her feet on the soil of Gevsilon, the air was quiet and still and damp. The line between the two was as sharp as if it had been sliced with a razor.

"I wouldn't recommend it, kid."

The voice was a stranger's, speaking the local trade pidgin. Eyo knew he was addressing her, but kept her gaze fixed on the boundary before her, and the maelstrom of sand beyond. She didn't care what some stranger thought.

People came here sometimes. Not the Oneui—not usually—but their neighbors in Gevsilon, or other residents of Driftwood looking for that rare thing, a quiet place to sit and be alone. The winds looked like their shrieking should drown out even thought, but their sound didn't cross the border, any more than the sand did. As long as you didn't look at the sandstorm, this place was peaceful.

But apparently the stranger didn't want to be quiet and alone. In her peripheral vision she saw movement, someone coming to stand at her side, not too close. Someone as tall as an Oneui adult, and that was unusual in Driftwood.

"You wouldn't be the first of your people to try," he said. "You're one of the Oneui, right? You must have heard the stories."

Oh, she had. It started as a dry, stinging wind, after their world parched to dust. Then it built into a sandstorm, one that raged for days without pause, just as their prophecies had foretold. Eyo's grandparents and the others of their town had refused to believe it was the end of the world; in their desperation, they gathered up their water and food and tied themselves together to prevent anyone from getting lost, and they went in search of a place safe from the sand.

They stumbled into Gevsilon. And that was how they found out their world *had* ended.

But not entirely. This remnant of it survived. And Gevsilon, their inward neighbor, had gone through an apocalypse of its own: a plague that rendered all their people sterile. There weren't many of the Nigevi left anymore, which meant there was enough room for the Oneui to resettle. Just a stone's throw from the remnants of their own world, and everything they'd left behind.

Of course some of them tried to go back. The first few returned coughing and blind, defeated by the ever-worsening storm. The next few stumbled out bloody, their clothing shredded and their flesh torn raw.

The last few didn't return at all.

"Why do you lot keep trying?" the stranger asked. "You know by now that it won't end well. Is this just how your people have taken to committing suicide?"

Some worlds did that, Eyo knew. Their people couldn't handle the realization that it was over, that Driftwood was their present and their future, until the last scraps of their world shrank and faded away. They killed themselves singly or en masse, making a ritual of it, a show of obedience to or protest against the implacable forces that sent them here.

Not her.

She meant to go on ignoring the stranger. It wasn't any of his business why she was here, staring at the lethal swirls of the sandstorm. But when she turned to go, she saw him properly: a tall man, slender and strong, his hair and eyes and fingernails pure black, but his skin tinged lightly with blue.

In Driftwood, people came in all sizes and colors and number of limbs and presence or lack of horns and tails. Eyo didn't claim to know them all. But she'd heard of only one person fitting this man's description.

"You're Last," she said. Sudden excitement made her tense.

His eyes tightened in apprehension, and he retreated a careful step. "I am."

"You can help me," Eyo said.

He retreated again, glancing over his shoulder, toward the faceless wall of the Oneui tenements, and the nearest opening past them. "I don't think so, kid. Sorry. I—"

She stepped forward, matching him. She didn't have her full growth yet, but she was quick and good at running; she would chase him if he fled. "You're a guide, aren't you? Someone who knows things, knows where to find things."

He stopped. "I—yes. I am."

One of the best in Driftwood, or so people said. He knew the patchwork of realities that made up this area, because he'd been around for longer than any of them. The stories claimed he was called Last because he was the last of his own world—a world that had been gone longer than anyone could remember.

Clarity dawned. "Oh. You thought I was going to ask you to go into the sandstorm?"

He gave the howling storm a sideways glance. "You wouldn't be the first."

Because the stories also said he couldn't die. Eyo scowled. "Someone asked you? Who? Tell me their name. I don't care what the storm is like; the idea of sending an *outsider* in there, asking them to bring back the—"

She cut herself off, but not before Last's eyebrows rose. "Bring back? You lost something in the storm?"

"It isn't lost," Eyo snapped. "We know exactly where it is."

Now she saw clarity dawn for *him*. "That's why your people keep going in," he said thoughtfully, gaze drifting sideways again. "Look, whatever it is—it may not even be there anymore. This is Driftwood; things crumble and fade away, even without apocalyptic sandstorms to scour them into dust."

Conviction stiffened Eyo's crest, her scalp feathers rising in a proud line. "Not this. Everything else will fall apart and die, but not—" She swallowed and shook her head. "When we are gone, this will remain."

His shrug said he didn't agree, but he also didn't

care enough to argue anymore. "So if you don't want to send me into that, what *do* you want me for?"

Eyo smoothed her crest with one hand, as flat to her skull as she could make it. If he knew her people, he would recognize that as a gesture of humility and supplication. "I want you to help me find a way to survive the sand."

"I told you it wouldn't work!"

In his fury, Last kicked the wall, which earned him a swift glare from Uaru. Eyo's grandaime had helped build this tenement with their own hands after the Oneui fled the sands. If Last broke something, they would take it out of his hide.

He gestured in apology, and Uaru went back to bandaging Eyo's fingers, their touches as gentle as possible. Eyo bit her lips until she was sure she could speak without hissing in pain. "You said it *probably* wouldn't work. I had to make sure."

"By sticking your hand across the border and letting it get torn apart? Use some common sense, In-Eyo! Get yourself a hunk of meat, wrap *that* up in the slidecloth, and see how it fares before you risk your own flesh!"

She hadn't thought of that. Her hand throbbed under Uaru's ministrations, as if in reproach. By the Oneui's best guess at keeping their old calendar, Eyo was an adult now; she'd gone through her rite of passage two triple cycles of Gevsilon's moons ago, with Uaru and Eyo's other hanaime kin drumming and singing the traditional songs. But Last still called her In-Eyo, as if she were a child, and it was hard to tell him to stop when she'd just done something that proved him right.

"I'll be more careful next time," she said.

Last scowled. "If you had any sense of self-preservation, there wouldn't *be* a next time. In-Eyo—Sa-Uaru—won't one of you tell me what's in there? What are you so desperate to retrieve?"

Uaru pressed their lips together and shook their head. They'd been furious when they found out the person who asked Last to go into the storm was another hanaime, Aune. But even Aune hadn't told Last what they were looking for—not after he refused to go.

Eyo's hand was fully bandaged. She cradled it gently after Uaru released her and began putting away their supplies. "It's something important, Sa-Last. Something we need. Our people never would have left it there if they'd realized . . ."

Her throat closed, ending the sentence. *If they'd realized they could never go back.*

She'd grown up on stories of all the things her grandparents had left behind, everything from shell cameos of ancestors she'd never met to her grandfather's favorite chair. The things they brought with them had the aura of holy relics—even the mundane ones, like the battered tin cup out of which Eyo's grandaime drank their salt tea every morning. But one absence loomed larger than all the rest, not because people spoke of it so often, but because they *didn't*.

Last turned away and braced his palms against the wall, head down. Eyo's hand throbbed again as he watched him. Finally, breathing out a long sigh, he said, "I'll keep looking. Slidecloth obviously isn't enough to protect you. And you would have been walking blind anyway, with that over your eyes. You need something better."

"Thank you," Eyo said.

He straightened up, his air of determination returning. "Thank me by being less reckless with the next possibility."

But the next possibility, when it came, couldn't be tested with a piece of meat.

Last handed over the package with something less than confidence. "You know, normally when a Sut-kef-chid is trying to sell you something, they praise its qualities to the skies. When she heard what I wanted this for, though, she got a *lot* less enthusiastic."

Eyo unwrapped the cloth, revealing a small ceramic flute. "This should calm the winds?"

"It *does* calm winds. And it works outside of Sutke; I tested it. But whether it's strong enough to overcome the sandstorm . . . the only way to find that out is to test it."

Which meant playing the flute. While standing in the storm.

Last's hand twitched. He clearly regretted giving her the flute. Eyo said, "I'm not as foolish as I used to be. Can you get me more slidecloth?"

It wouldn't protect her against the winds for long; she'd proved that three lunar years ago. But it could buy her some time. "I'll see what I can do," Last said.

Wrapped in slidecloth, with a rope harness tied around her body and the flute in her hand, Eyo faced the sandstorm again. Someone had built a bridge over what remained of the Eckuoz Sea at the beginning of the last solar year, widdershins of Oneua and Gevsilon; it turned the weed-filled gap between the windowless backs of the Oneui tenements and the sandstorm into a thoroughfare for people in that part of Driftwood. Garbed and harnessed as she was, Eyo garnered a lot of odd stares from passersby. Last held the other end of the rope, ready to pull.

"Give me a hundred heartbeats," she said.

Last snorted. "What am I, a fishmonger with a day-old catch? No bargaining. I'll give you thirty, and I'll pull you out sooner if I see the slidecloth start to shred. You're already going to get your face flayed." Unhappiness weighed down his words.

There was no arguing with him. Short of taking the rope harness off entirely, she couldn't prevent him from yanking her back. Eyo's younger self might have done it in a fit of bravado, but she was smart enough now to accept the precaution. "All right."

She pulled the slidecloth mask down over her face, leaving only her mouth clear. Somehow, not being able to see the storm made it far more frightening. Her pulse pounded, counting off the beats faster than usual. Eyo's breath shallowed, and when she brought the flute to her lips, it took her three tries to produce a sound, even though she'd practiced for this day.

Gevsilon never had much of a breeze, as if the forces that brought Driftwood together needed some cosmic counterbalance for the maelstrom of Oneua. What movement there was died as Eyo began to play, the air settling around her like a warm, damp blanket.

She wasn't ready. But she made herself step forward anyway.

The list of things that didn't work grew longer as the years went by.

Slidecloth didn't last long enough. The flute might

have worked, but the winds tore away Eyo's breath before she could produce a note, and when she tried going back with a slidecloth-covered barrel over her head as shelter, the flute only affected the air inside the barrel. Then Uaru had to pick splinters out of her cheek after the barrel shattered. A potion whose seller swore it would make her invulnerable turned out to be nothing more than flavored wine. Someone else legitimately had the ability to turn Eyo insubstantial, but that would have made it impossible for her to do anything else—like carry an object. Burrowing underground kept her safe from the storm; unfortunately, she could spend the rest of her life digging tunnels and never find what she was looking for, not without some way to orient herself. Flying could lift her above the winds, but that didn't change the fact that she would have to descend into them eventually. Remembering her grandparents' stories of how the world dried out before the storm began, Eyo even looked into the possibility of channeling the remnants of the Eckuoz Sea across the border into Oneua, on the principle that it might lay the dust. But a broken dam in Ishlt left the aquatic Leshir in desperate search of a new home, and they took up residence in the waters of Eckuoz before Eyo could put that particular crack-brained idea to the test.

Last showed up intermittently, whenever he found some new prospect for Eyo to consider. Sometimes his absence stretched out to a solar year or more. But she never had any doubt that she would see him again; the possibility of him losing interest was as inconceivable as his death.

He never offered to go into the storm for her. And she never asked.

She worked as a trader, primarily among the Brenak'i, where her scarred face and hand earned her respect. When Eyo was young, the prospect of being a hero to her people had consumed all her thoughts; as the years passed, it slipped further and further into the back of her mind, pushed aside by duties and opportunities more immediate.

But it never went away. And when her daughter was born, it came roaring back to life, as if it had never faded at all.

Ila wasn't her first. Eyo had an older child-pair, a boy and a hanaime, sired by an Oneui lover. But even if her second birth hadn't been single—a rarity among her people—the girl's appearance would have told everyone her father was an outsider, her eyes too small, her face too round, her skin more Brenak'i gold than Oneui red. She had scalp feathers, but none along the backs of her arms.

"It happens with almost everyone, sooner or later," Last said one night as they sat outside. All three of Gevsilon's moons were in the sky, making what the Nigevi had called "false day;" people went about their business in the half-light, but the strip of packed dirt between the tenements and the border was much less busy than usual. "Some peoples manage to keep themselves completely separate until they're gone, and a few seem to be fertile only with their own kind, but most wind up mixing with other races in Driftwood."

About half the inhabitants of Gevsilon these days were Drifters, the descendants of such cross-world encounters. Products of a hundred worlds, they had no world but Driftwood itself. "It all goes away in the end," Eyo said, her voice thick. "Ila's great-grandchildren will be Drifters. They'll know nothing of Oneua." Then she pounded her fist against the dirt. "I say that as if *I* know anything about it. All I know are my grandparents' stories! I was born after they fled here. We try to live as they did before, but it isn't the same. We eat the food of the Brenak'i, wear fabric the Thiwd make from worms. Without our suns we can't count time correctly, so all our rituals are guesses. If we had—"

She swallowed the words before they could come out. Last nodded. "If you had whatever it is you left behind."

He'd given up on asking her what it was. But he hadn't given up on finding her a way.

Eyo let her head sag. "I know it won't fix anything. Everything in Driftwood fades eventually; the Oneui will be no different. Generations from now, that storm will be gone, and some other dying world will have taken our place. But what happens before then—that still matters. At least to me."

Last stroked the white feathers of her crest. There was no one else she allowed to make such an intimate gesture anymore, now that Uaru had passed away. Last wasn't kin—she didn't even know what world he'd come from—but somewhere during these years of effort, he had become family.

"I'll keep searching," he said. "For you."

Driftwood took, and took, and took—but it also gave.

Ila was growing like a weed and Eyo's eldest pair had passed their rites of adulthood when Last appeared with news from the Edge. "You have something," Eyo said, hope flaring in her heart.

He'd had something before, countless times. But usually he looked optimistic, or maybe skeptical. This time he looked grim. And that, against all logic, gave her hope.

"I do," Last said, the words dragging with reluctance. "But it—hellfire. Eyo, it's something they do to their *criminals*."

In Driftwood, customs of punishment varied as much as anything else. For all Eyo knew, criminals in this newly arrived world were made to wear outlandish costumes, or eat foul-smelling herbs. "I don't care. Whatever it is, I'll—"

Last put up his hand before she could finish her sentence. "Don't. I almost didn't even come tell you, except . . . I can't do that to you. Can't lie. I've always brought you everything, and so I have to bring this. But it's *permanent*, Eyo. Assuming it even works here, you won't be able to come back from it. And I can't swear that it will help you. I don't know what it is you need to retrieve from Oneua, but you might do this to yourself and then find you aren't able to bring that thing out like you want."

"Sa-Last." The formal address brought him up short. Eyo laid her hands over his and said, "Tell me."

He'd lived for a long time. More lifetimes than anyone could count, him included, Eyo thought. Somewhere in all those ages, he'd learned how to spit out bad news without choking on it.

"They turn their criminals into wind."

Her fingers went slack.

Wind.

Like the never-ending storm in Oneua.

"*Self-aware* wind," Last said. "You'll still be yourself. You'll know where you are, and be able to move as you wish. And if what you're looking for is small enough, you might be able to pick it up and blow it to the border. But you'll be like that *forever*, Eyo— until Oneua is gone."

Her heart seemed to have gone silent in her chest. *If what you're looking for is small enough.* It was—oh, it was.

Which meant that if this worked—if these new-comers to Driftwood could change her into wind—if she could find her way into the sanctuary—if she could control herself well enough—

Then she would die. Her mind would linger, but as far as her people were concerned, she would be gone. Lost forever in the storm that had consumed Oneua, until Driftwood finally ground the last of it out of existence.

Eyo said, "Ila is still a child."

Someone else might have thought she was preparing to refuse. But Last knew the Oneui: once Ila passed her rites, Eyo's obligations to her half-Brenak'i daughter would be done.

And he knew Eyo.

If the air of Gevsilon hadn't been so still, so quiet, she wouldn't have heard his words. "How long?"

"Two lunar years," Eyo said.

Last nodded. "I'll be ready when the time comes. But if you change your mind—"

They both knew she wouldn't.

No one had come to watch her previous attempts. People who thought they could go back into Oneua were eccentrics at best, lunatics at worst; the polite thing to do was to turn a blind eye.

But when the day came that Eyo faced the border

for the final time, the tenements emptied, and the well-trammeled thoroughfare from the dwindling Eckuoz Lake was filled with the silent, watching ranks of Oneui.

Last stood a pace from the border with their visitor, a magistrate from the distant world called Tzuh. If this one was any example, the Tz were a short, stocky people, the least airy beings Eyo could imagine. Last referred to the magistrate as "they," so Eyo thought of them as hanaime, though in truth they had no more gender than a rock—at least that she'd been told. She hadn't spoken much to them. Right now, all her thoughts were bent on her own people.

The eldest hanaime among them performed the rites: a funeral for one who would soon be dead. Stripped bare, her skin covered in an intricate lace of white paint, Eyo turned to face the border—and was caught halfway through her turn by Ila, flinging her arms around her mother's waist in defiance of all custom.

"I love you," Ila whispered into her shoulder, fierce through the tears. "And I will remember. Every bit of it. I'll teach my children about Oneua, and they will teach theirs, from now until the end of Driftwood."

Eyo laid her cheek atop her daughter's head. The promise was as impossible as it was heartfelt. This was the truth of Driftwood: that in the end, everything went away and was forgotten, no matter how hard people tried to cling to the scraps.

But the effort still meant something.

"Wait for me at the border," Eyo said back, stroking her daughter's crest. "I will bring it to you—I swear."

Then she pried Ila away, gently, and approached Last and the Tz magistrate.

Last met her gaze. *He* understood, she thought. He of all people would.

He murmured a phrase in a language she didn't recognize. His own native tongue? It had the sound of a blessing. Then he stepped back and it was just the magistrate, who set their feet against the ground and began a series of clicking noises that seemed to slip between the pieces that made up Eyo, separating them, slicing the bonds between them until they all came apart—

An instant before she became entirely insubstantial, Last placed his hands against her back and *shoved.*

The storm was never-ending insanity.

Particles of sand tore through Eyo, robbed of their power to harm her. But she cartwheeled through the air without any sense of up or down, left or right; there was only *forward*, borne along on the ever-changing currents. *Backward* did not exist at all. In the face of such fury, even the thought was impossible.

She could not fight the wind, any more than she had been able to withstand it before. In order to survive, she had to join with it. And in order to win passage through, she had to ride the torrent.

Forward, forward, always forward, swirling and veering and tearing across a landscape she knew only from her grandparents' stories. Everything was worn down by the constant friction of the sand, rounding into smooth shapes she could barely identify. Then it would all vanish, as she arced upward and away and lost track of where she was.

But gradually she learned.

And even more gradually, she began to work her way toward her goal.

It was slow progress. Sometimes she wound up farther away than before, her own strength nothing against the power of the storm. But Eyo had learned patience, in her years of trying to enter Oneua. She simply rode the winds away, then came back for another pass. She found spaces between the crumbling buildings where the fury was quieter. She mapped out the vortices where everything became chaos, and found there was pattern within it after all.

And then, one night when both of Oneua's suns had set, she slipped inside the hollow wreck of a building whose sand-scoured walls still bore the unmistakable tint of green jade.

The winds had broken open doors, windows, roofs. But not floors, not yet—and in here, where only a portion of the storm could reign, Eyo's hard-won skill bore fruit. In a single instinctive movement she was across the entry chamber, into the inner room, at the entrance to a spiral staircase winding downward. The storm itself aided her now, dragging her down that spiral, but she almost missed the opening at the bottom, flinging her insubstantial form through it by the narrowest of margins.

Here the air was almost still. The place was as dark as Last's hair; no flame had illuminated it since the Oneui fled. But a wind did not need eyes to see. Eyo spread herself out, floating along at a pace of her own choosing, farther and farther from the reach of the storm. Soon hers was the only movement, drifting past a double rank of statues whose lines were as crisp and unworn as the day they were first carved. They seemed to watch her go by, and Eyo offered up a silent prayer to them, that she would not have done all this in vain.

She had not.

It sat in a shallow bowl of gold, untouched by the distant wind. A single feather: the most holy relic of her people, taken from the crest of Ona, foremother of their race. Too precious and fragile to risk in the storm, the feather had remained behind when the Oneui fled, because they didn't realize they would never be able to return for it.

Eyo could move a feather.

But could she keep it safe from the storm?

She gathered it up with the lightest touch, wafting it on a breath of air to the center of herself. She would have only one opportunity: once she re-entered the tempest, there would be no chance to retreat and try again. If she lost control of the feather, or let the sand rip through her and her precious burden . . .

Waiting would not make her any more ready. Eyo wrapped herself around the feather, prayed, and launched herself back into the wind.

A balcony lined the back wall of the Oneui settlement in Gevsilon, facing the border.

It had changed a great deal from the early years. Children now played on the open ground in their idle moments, and laundry often hung from the balcony's railing. Still, the place had a touch of the sacred to it, and from time to time anyone who came out there would pause in their work or play and gaze at the border with Oneua, the unabated fury of the storm just a short distance away. Moss and flowers grew in the space between, since the thoroughfare had been blocked up.

Ila sat in her accustomed spot just a pace away from that silent, sand-torn barrier. Waiting.

A bell rang near the center of Gevsilon. She'd

grown accustomed to the sound since the Wilsl moved in, taking the place of the now-extinct Nigevi. Soon one of the children would bring her food, and brush her hair, and talk with her for a little while before leaving her to her vigil.

She never troubled herself to wonder what would happen after she was gone. Her mother had promised to bring the feather to her. Ila's faith was absolute.

Something swirled by in the sand and was gone.

Ila rose, so quickly her aging bones protested. Had she imagined it. . . ?

Then it came again. Without hesitation, she plunged her hand through the intangible barrier, from one world into the next, and took hold of what she'd seen.

She expected to feel sand tear the skin from her hand, the flesh from her bones. Instead she felt a brief, soft caress—and then, before the storm could take her, Ila pulled her hand back.

Slowly, not daring to breathe, she uncurled her fingers. Ona's crest feather balanced in her palm, iridescent and gold.

Tears slipped down Ila's cheeks. "Thank you," she whispered to the storm, then turned to face the Oneui. As they knelt in a rippling wave, she raised the feather high above her head.

Eyo had kept her promise.

recorded by Yilime

The Peacemaker

"**Y**OU SKIPPED OVER part of the story."

Ioi stares at Kuondae. "What do you mean?"

The feline woman turns to sit cross-legged on the wall, facing the seats of the amphitheater, and spreads her arms. "What about Last? It's a touching story and all about your grandmother—but aren't we here for him? What happened to *him*?"

That is, after all, the question that has brought everyone to the amphitheater. Either to have it answered . . . or to grieve for the answer they believe is true.

But Kuondae's meaning is more specific. "After Eyo went into the wind," she says patronizingly, omitting the Oneui honorific "Sa-" on purpose. "What did Last do?"

"He waited," Ioi says.

"For how long?"

Ioi's feet shift uneasily. "Nine days."

"At the expense of his hosts, no doubt. I knew your mother Ila; she would have fed and housed him, grateful that he booted her mother into a sandstorm at her request." Kuondae scratches lazily in the thin fuzz of her skin. "And then what did he do?"

Ioi's answer is barely audible even to those nearby. "He left."

"He left," Kuondae repeats, loud enough for all to hear. "And did he ever come back? Does he even know Eyo brought her precious feather out of the storm?"

"It took *years*," Ioi said hotly. "Most people thought my mother was a fool for waiting. But Eyo—"

"This isn't about Eyo, is it? It's about Last, and your claim that he was driven by friendship." Kuondae slinks off the wall again and begins to pace, back and forth in front of Ioi.

They have a crowd now. The scattered observers have thickened, their numbers augmented by passersby and word going through the Shreds, that what started as a pile of remembrances and doubts is now a storytelling performance. Even some of the Oneui are there, and looking like they might rip into Kuondae if she keeps talking. One of Eyo's shed crest-feathers sits alongside Ona's in the new shrine they've built in Gevsilon; an insult to her is an insult to all their people.

But it's Last that Kuondae is insulting, and the amphitheater is neutral ground, belonging to nobody. There aren't any laws that bind all Drifters, just customs and habits, but to attack her would be a shocking breach of both. Kuondae knows it, and warms to her theme. "This man," she says. "This *immortal* man, if we're to believe the stories about him. This man who has outlived not only his own world, but hundreds of others, never found the time to come back to Gevsilon and see how his old friend was doing—if she'd succeeded in her quest."

Lazr-iminya is still there, sitting next to Eshap, who holds her knobbled hand in both of his. Now she puffs a breath at Kuondae and says something that makes the feline woman snarl.

"Speak up!" someone calls down.

At Lazr-iminya's nudge, Eshap stands and turns to face the crowd. "She said, 'Just because you don't have enough heart to understand grief doesn't mean we're all as cold as you.'"

"He's not dead!" The words burst out of a small kid: Dreceyl, older than he looks but still not very old. He stamps his foot and then runs down to the stage. "How can people think Last is dead? He's survived *everything*."

A clamor fills the amphitheater, which until that point has been more or less respectfully silent. If there's one thing capable of thriving in Driftwood, it's rumors, and in the days since word went around that Last was gone, this one has grown a hundred heads.

He went into the Crush. He traveled to the Edge and leapt off into the Mist. He committed suicide with a weapon that before its world's apocalypse had been used to kill a god. He ate or drank something that turned out to be poison to his kind. The final artifact of his world was caught for ages in the depths of the Crush, but now it's finally vanished, and it took Last with it.

The whole thing was never true in the first place. The stories about Last were just that: stories. He was never immortal; at best there was just a long series of men who looked enough like the stories to pass. And now he's gone, just like everything else in Driftwood.

What began as a silent memorial and then became a tribute starts shredding into chaos. Dreceyl shoves Kuondae, who to him is just a disrespectful stranger. She hisses at him and raises a hand, but Ioi stops her from striking, which brings the Oneui in; Ioi may be only one-quarter of their blood, but Kuondae's provocation has temporarily erased that gap. In the stands above, people begin to shout competing theories, points and counterpoints, few of them backed by solid facts. The dark-skinned woman with the gold wound into her hair watches silently, leaning against the crumbling sandstone wall with her jaw set hard. The man in the robe sets his pen down and waits.

A powerful bellow finally cuts through the noise. It comes from Febrenew, who has emerged from behind his tables of food and drink with a cylindrical leather case.

He outmasses Kuondae by three to one, and she backs away when he glares her down. To Dreceyl, who often runs errands for him, Febrenew says, "Give me a hand, here."

With Dreceyl's assistance he pulls off the leather cap, then removes and unrolls a large scroll of paper. Febrenew lays it out on the amphitheater's floor, weighing its corners down with a few pieces of fruit Dreceyl fetches from his makeshift bar.

Curiosity is a powerful force. By the time Febrenew is done, he has something approximating the quiet Eshap enjoyed. People crane their necks and murmur when they recognize the paper; some of them come down to the low wall at the bottom of the stands to get a better look.

"This isn't the original," Febrenew booms. He doesn't need architectural help to make his voice carry. "That's long gone, along with the bar it used to hang in. But there are three promises every one of us has made, when we take over the job I hold now. The first is to keep the name: Spit in the Crush's Eye. The second is to set up again somewhere else if the place we're using goes away. And the third . . ."

He looks around the amphitheater, making eye contact with people here and there. "The third," he says, "is to keep copying this map. And to remember where it came from."

The Ascent of Unreason

"**I** WANT TO make a map of Driftwood."

Watching Last cough up his wine at the words wasn't the *only* reason for Tolyat's declaration, but he had to admit it was part of the appeal. The man was a guide, and had seen so much, experienced so much, gone so many places, that it was hard to crack his shell of burnt-out weariness. One pretty much had to say something so outrageous it should never be uttered by a sane man.

Tolyat leaned back, and nearly fell out of his hammock. They were in Kyey, where the local people had given over most of what remained of their world to the cultivation of some plant with an unpronounceable name, whose chief virtue was the production of tough fiber. The Kyeyi ate a little of it, sold a lot, and used the rest to make practically everything around them. Even the walls were mostly fiber, woven between the occasional piece of imported timber.

Despite coughing, Last balanced on his hammock like he'd been born Kyeyi. He wiped his chin and set his wine horn on the table—more fiber, mixed with mud and baked hard. Even the *wine* was a byproduct of that damned plant, from the liquid drained off during fiber extraction. Tolyat thought it tasted like fermented rope, but Last, for some inexplicable reason, liked it.

Last said, "Only idiots bother trying to make maps of Driftwood."

"So I'm an idiot. I still want to do it."

"Listen, Tolyat—"

He swiped Last's wine horn before the other could pick it up. "I know what comes next. You're going to dip your fingers in this stuff and start drawing on the table, little concentric circles, Mist, Edge, Ring, Shreds, and then the Crush at the middle, and tell me that's the only useful map anyone can make. Who said I was trying to be *useful?*"

Last's black eyes narrowed in skepticism, but a glimmer of curiosity broke through. "Then what are you trying to be?"

Tolyat fiddled with the wine horn, rubbing his thumb over the rough place where the rim had chipped. The translucent material was almost the same orange-honey color as the scales of his skin. It wasn't a color he saw often, not anymore. Not since he'd left his own world, losing himself in the study of Driftwood and its patchwork composition.

He wanted to have a meaningful answer to Last's question. Partly for his own satisfaction, but even more as a gift to his friend. Some kind of grand philosophical mission, something that would push back, if only for a moment, against the inescapable nihilism of this place. They lived surrounded by death, and it was easy to fall, as Last had, into apathy and despair.

He could try saying something noble. Something about how how mapping the face of Driftwood—even if the map would be obsolete before they could blink—would preserve this moment for future generations and worlds to know.

Instead he told the truth. "I just think it would be fun."

Last's dark eyebrows rose. Tolyat found those lines of hair endlessly entertaining; they expressed so many emotions. In this case, it was a mix of disbelief and weary resignation. "Fun. Do you have any idea how long that would take? Going from world to world, dealing with all the language barriers, all the different customs, hoping the air the next block over will still be something you can breathe—not to mention figuring out what standard of measurement you should use." He shook his head. "I may be good at what I do, Tolyat, but even I don't know *all* of Driftwood. You'd need an army of guides, and a longer lifespan than your race has got. What are you grinning at?"

The grin had been spreading during Last's entire speech, until Tolyat felt he could barely hold the laughter in. Rather than answer, he fished in his pockets, pulling out two small stone discs. He stacked them atop one another, smooth faces up, placing both on the table. "Ever seen these before?"

Last peered at their pearlescent surfaces. It wouldn't have surprised Tolyat if he said he had; sometimes it really seemed the guide had seen *everything*. But he shook his head.

Still with the grin, Tolyat said, "Watch this."

When he flipped the topmost disc, smooth side down, it no longer sat atop its mate. Instead it rose into the air, perhaps a handspan—Tolyat's handspan; two of Last's—above the table.

Last shrugged, unimpressed. "Magnets. So?"

"Not magnets. Something better. I bought them from Etthril in Flatwall, but they come from a place called Bhauin, a bit Edgeward of Ik. A girl there has rediscovered the secret of making them, if you can believe that; for once, something in this place has been learned, rather than lost. But she can make them bigger. And stronger."

Still, Last frowned. "What has that got to do with mapping?"

Tolyat thought the grin might actually split his face open, like the old carvings of the demon Sevot, back in his home world. Split it open, and let his excitement come pouring out. "I'm not going to go through Driftwood. I'm going to go above it."

Boundaries between worlds were unpredictable about what they stopped, and what they allowed through. Weather usually didn't pass beyond its home world. Rivers sometimes ended at the border, sometimes flowed on through to flood a neighboring ghetto. Sound usually went, but not always; Tolyat didn't hear the singing—if he could call it singing—until he stepped across the border into Bhauin. "What is *that?*"

Last, he suspected, had taken it as a personal affront that Tolyat had known something he didn't. Which was actually encouraging, though Tolyat would never admit it; he'd seen more life in the man these past few days than he had in ages. Last had roused enough to hunt down every bit of information he could find about this Shred—and when he put his mind to it, he was a *very* good hunter. "Didn't I mention?" Last said. "There's a religious revival underway."

Those were rarely good. In Driftwood, a "religious revival" usually meant that some self-proclaimed messiah had convinced people they could save themselves, and their world, by killing whoever the messiah didn't like. The inhabitants of a neighboring

Shred, perhaps—or any stranger who wandered in. "Should we be here?"

"Don't worry. That girl you mentioned, who makes the stones? They've decided she's blessed by the gods. A prophesied leader, come to save them." Last shrugged, his expression wry. "Not that they ever *had* any prophecies before now; they imported that idea from Ik. Anyway, it's all very happy and optimistic. No killing required. Though what they'll do when you ask to buy stones, I don't know. How many do you need?"

While Last had researched Bhauin, Tolyat had tried to do calculations. He didn't get very far: there were too many variables, most of them obscure to him. How powerful could the girl make the stones? Over what range could they operate? At least he'd verified that they worked in every Shred he'd tried; their repelling force seemed to translate across borders. But he couldn't admit he didn't know. "A dozen pairs, maybe. More wouldn't be a bad thing."

"A dozen." Last blew a slow breath out. "Well, let's see what the prophesied leader has to say."

The Bhauish notion of singing involved alternating between a strident ululation and a series of harsh caws. There seemed to be a pattern to it; Tolyat thought he had almost worked it out by the time Last got the prophesied leader to stop ululating and cawing in his face. She was a tiny thing, even more so than the rest of her race, and pale as blood; she looked like a juvenile, but she listened attentively enough when Last spoke in the local pidgin. "You make these stones?"

They didn't know what the Bhauish called the things, so Tolyat reluctantly brought out his pair, to illustrate. A murmur ran through the gathered crowd, which sounded hostile to his wary ears.

Last heard it, too, but he made a business out of taking people into hostile Shreds, and bringing them back out again. When the girl growled something half-intelligible about how the stones shouldn't be spread outside of Bhauin, Last was unfazed. "These have gone through the hands of half a dozen merchants; they've been outside your world for nearly two of your years. How long ago did you regain the gift of making them?"

Her answer was easier to make out. "At moonrise."

Tolyat glanced up, saw an enormous crescent of cobalt blue hanging in the sky above them. That told him nothing; lunar cycles varied wildly between worlds. But Bhauish astronomy was apparently one of the things Last had picked up on his hunt, because he said, "See? Your goddesses aren't angry that it was sold. Maybe they *want* Bhauish stones to be spread to other worlds. This fellow here would like to be your first customer." He pointed at Tolyat, who smiled and hoped the Bhauish weren't a race who read things like that as a sign of aggression.

They didn't seem to be. The prophet-girl muttered

to one of her companions in a language that sounded like the cawing from a moment before, then turned back to Last and Tolyat with an expression that could only be called predatory. Suppressing a sigh, Tolyat braced himself for some hard bargaining.

The first time Tolyat flipped over one of the new shauein stones, it went through the ceiling of his room and cracked the cross-timber of the roof one story above. When he scrambled up there to grab it, the stone was all but glued to the wood, trying to force itself still higher, and his upstairs neighbor was less than amused at the delight on Tolyat's face.

He conducted a second test in the caverns of Neggaeph, first building a scaffold he could wheel around to retrieve any levitating stones from the ceiling. With the figures from that, he sat down to calculate just how this plan would work.

Last sprawled across one of the curved stone couches that lined the wall and watched him work for a few minutes. Then he spoke, in a tone that was far too carefully neutral. "You realize you'll have to place yourself near the Crush."

"I know." Tolyat had thought of that ages ago, before he ever showed the shauien pair to Last—but it didn't prevent his stylus from skidding a little, gouging an errant line in the wax of his tablet.

Observing that, Last said, "Despite what people think, it can't pull you in."

"I know." Which was true, but irrelevant to his nerves. The Crush was the black heart of Driftwood, a tangled, broken mass of fragments too small to call worlds. Everything went there in the end. Unsurprisingly, few people in Driftwood liked to talk about it, and nobody wanted to go anywhere near it. When a world drew close, any inhabitants it might have left generally abandoned the place, losing themselves in the sea of cross-bred Drifters who belonged to no world.

But it *was* the center point, as near as anybody could tell. If Tolyat wanted to see the whole of Driftwood at once, he had to be close to the Crush.

He bent his head over his tablet once more, carving careful figures with the stylus. Last let him work in silence. When Tolyat finished, he said, "Eight should be enough—they're more powerful than I expected—though I'll install all twelve, just in case they weaken or a few get jarred loose. But I should be able to lift you, me, and the basket with just eight."

The eyebrows shot up again. Tolyat wondered what it must be like, having hairs on your face that advertised your every reaction. Last said, "*Who* and the basket?"

"You and me." Tolyat laid down his tablet and stylus. "You *are* coming with me, right?"

The world he chose for the launching point had two important lacks: people and wind.

It was, as Last had advised, close to the Crush—close enough that what little of it still existed had been abandoned quite some time ago. Nobody was around to object when Tolyat paid a pair of Ffes to knock down what remained of the only surviving building and flatten the ground, into which he set one half of each shauein pair. As for wind, none of the neighboring Shreds had storms that would spill over into this nameless world-fragment and threaten to knock the basket from its alignment above the stones.

By now the rumors had spread; half the population of the Shreds seemed to know that Tolyat the scholar was trying something mad, and most of them had come to watch. The prophesied leader of the Bhauish had taken an interest in the matter, and some of her people were keeping the mob away from Tolyat as he made his final preparations—or, more likely, keeping the mob away from their precious stones. But they parted to allow Last through, along with the cart he was dragging behind him.

Tolyat paused to stare. "What in the name of everybody else's god is *that?*"

"Backup." Last dropped the cart shafts, and a flounce of cloth spilled out the front. "Help me attach this to your basket."

"Not until you tell me what it is."

The guide sighed and stepped closer, lowering his voice so the watching crowd wouldn't hear. "You've heard the stories about me, right?"

"Stories?"

"The ones that say I can't die."

"Oh." Tolyat scratched his earhole in embarrassment. "Yes."

It was, he thought, the foundation of their friendship, or at least part of it: he never asked questions about Last. He'd given it some thought, back when they first met. If it was true that Last was immortal, that he was the one thing in Driftwood that didn't die, then the trick to it must not be anything he could share with other people; otherwise he would've been the richest man in any world. If it wasn't true, then the man was probably tired of people chasing after a secret he didn't have. Either way, there was no point in Tolyat asking.

But now Last had brought it up, and curiosity overwhelmed that logic. He couldn't resist saying, "Are those stories true?"

Last's mouth was set in a line that might have indicated either terror or suppressed hilarity. "I have no intention of giving you a chance to find out. The fabric's a big sack, open on one end; we attach it to the basket, with the open end down, and light this furnace underneath to fill it with hot air. Once it's full, we'll float."

Tolyat dropped his armful of fabric. "You want me to trust my life to magic floating hot air?"

"You're already trusting it to magic floating stones, aren't you? This works, trust me." Last shrugged. "Hasn't been used in Driftwood since Ad Aprinchenlin went into the Crush, but that doesn't mean it's a bad idea. Falling hurts, Tolyat—a *lot*. I'd rather have two things between me and the ground, not just one."

Grumbling, Tolyat helped. The sack was shaped like a bottle with a narrow neck; enormous as it was, he didn't trust the flimsy fabric to hold *anything*. But the weight was negligible, even with the furnace, and it seemed to make Last feel better.

Once the sack was in place, Tolyat turned around—and realized there was silence. The entire crowd was watching in breathless anticipation. They packed the narrow streets of the adjacent Shreds, peering out of windows and from rooftops of abandoned buildings, in every world-fragment but the even smaller ones that lay Crushward. And judging by their expressions, they wanted a speech.

He'd been too busy with calculations and the gathering of supplies to plan any kind of speech. "Um," Tolyat said, scratching his earhole again. It was Last's original question all over again, with him feeling like he ought to have something grand to say in response.

"I'm going to go make a map of Driftwood," he said. "As detailed as I can. Maybe you think that's a waste of time, and maybe you're right. But I'm going to do it anyway. So wish me luck—pray I don't die— and when I get back to the ground, I'll tell you what I saw."

And with that sorry attempt behind him, he turned and climbed into the basket.

Last was already inside. The thing wasn't very big; Tolyat could span it with his arms, and that damned sack and furnace took up most of the available space. The rest held his tools, the paper and ink and measuring devices he would use to draw his map. He had to root around beneath all that equipment and fabric to find the shauein stones set into the floor of woven Kyeyi fiber, mounted in rotating brackets.

"Ready?" he asked Last.

The guide still had that look, terror or hilarity. But whichever it was, it brought his black eyes alive. "Let's see what this place looks like from above."

On a counted signal, they each flipped one shauein stone, on opposite sides of the circular basket. This was part of why Tolyat wanted Last; he had to activate two pairs of stones at once, or the basket risked unbalancing, tipping him out onto the ground. With the repelling faces toward each other, the stones pushed away from their mates below, and the basket began to rise.

Only a little, and slowly. Which was fine by Tolyat. He had no desire to go shooting uncontrolled up into Driftwood's sky. He and Last each moved a quarter-turn around the basket's circumference; Tolyat dug beneath the slick fabric of the sack and found the next stone. Two more flipped, and the basket rose further. Now they were above the tallest buildings in the vicinity of the Crush, but glancing outside showed him various towers scattered around the huddled mass of the Shreds, and even something that looked like a broken bit of mountain. If he wanted to see the whole of Driftwood, they would have to go higher still.

Two more stones, and then two more. Eight pairs of shauein stones, pushing the basket into the sky, Tolyat's heart beating faster with every turn. He cast another glance through a gap in the woven side, frowning, trying to think. This was where his calculations became uncertain, and maybe the weight of that furnace was throwing them off. "Again," he said, and together he and Last flipped a ninth and then a tenth pair.

That should be high enough. Taking a deep breath, Tolyat stood up.

Or tried. To his embarrassment, it took him several long moments to convince his knees they wanted to support him. The basket's base was taut beneath his feet, but not rigid; he felt it give slightly as he shifted, and he was briefly paralyzed by the horrified certainty that the entire structure would rip apart beneath his weight and the pressure of the shauein stones. But finally, gripping the edge so hard it printed the weave into his unscaled palms, he stood.

And saw Driftwood.

The immensity of it knocked the breath from his lungs. Towers, plazas, haphazard housing blocks held up only by their neighbors. Water, glittering unexpectedly here and there among the structures. Clouds and fog and an irregular stretch of air filled with lightning. Lights of a hundred different colors, some coming from things that must be suns and moons and stars, others from no apparent source, because the celestial bodies from which they emanated were visible only from the ground to which they belonged.

His gaze swept across the collage of realities, from the mostly urban patchwork of the Shreds, through the Ring and outward to the Edge, where the newly Drifted worlds were large enough to still have mountains and forests, deserts and seas. Their details faded, his eye not sharp enough to make them out, and then beyond those lands. . . .

The dark, featureless expanse of the Mist. Out of which worlds came, convulsing in the throes of their doom, to finish dying in Driftwood.

Next to him, Last breathed a few soft words that might have been a prayer, or a curse.

Tolyat sucked in a shuddering gasp of air. Fun—he'd thought this would be fun. To fly in the air, like the enormous bats that had died out of his world when he was a child, like he'd always dreamed of doing. When he'd thought about what he would see, he thought in terms of maps: lines and images on paper, their labels to be gathered later, from Last and other guides.

He hadn't understood that he would see *Driftwood*. From the grey, empty sea of the Mist to the Crush itself.

As if drawn by a magnet, his gaze went down.

His heart gave a single, lurching thud when he looked at the ground; he couldn't tell how much of it was for the expanse of empty air below his feet, and how much for the Crush. From here, it looked like hardly anything: a tight knot of wreckage, everything ground too small to stand out at this distance. But he was staring straight into its heart, and this was it: this was where worlds died, gasping their last amid dust and broken trash.

Such a little space, to hold such terrible power.

Or maybe it had no power at all. He'd always thought of the Crush as some kind of vortex, sucking things in and grinding them up. Now, flying high above the motley face of Driftwood, he saw it differently: saw the Mist, vomiting out pieces of worlds, which scraped and pushed against one another, forcing their neighbors inward, like a millstone crushing grain. *We destroy each other,* Tolyat thought, and for a moment he stopped breathing again.

What restored air to his lungs was the sense that neither image was true. Or maybe both were. Driftwood wasn't simple, and it didn't accept simple explanations. It held whole universes of contradiction within its bounds, and maybe this was one more, that the destructive force came from both directions and from neither. Whatever brought or sent worlds to this purgatorial end, it wasn't the Crush, and it wasn't the Mist, and it wasn't the people caught in between.

But when Tolyat looked down again, he found that the Crush no longer frightened him. He took several slow breaths, then turned to face Last.

The guide was stone-still, his face completely unreadable. Even his eyebrows gave nothing away. Water glimmered upon his high cheekbones, traced the edge of his jaw; Tolyat had seen a similar thing among other races, and with most of them it signaled great emotion. Grief, or joy, or fear: tears seemed very contradictory things. He couldn't tell what they meant now. But Last, sensing Tolyat's gaze upon him, turned his head and answered with a small, oddly serene smile.

"I've lived a damn long time," he said, "and seen more of Driftwood than most . . . but I've never seen this. Thank you."

It was as if the shauein stones had lifted some

great weight from his spirit. Tolyat felt it, too: up here, with all of Driftwood spread out below them, it was impossible to be dragged down by the mundanity of life. That weight might return with their descent . . . but for now, they were free.

Tolyat nodded. And then, because the moment was too intense to bear any longer, he bent and picked up his paper.

With a board underneath braced against the basket's edge, he began to draw. Outlines first; his eye sought out the places where the air changed, or the architecture, or something else that heralded a boundary between worlds. Last identified the places he knew, and Tolyat marked the names with tiny, careful letters. An unending series of names, many of them hard to spell with any of the writing systems he knew; he did his best, then moved on. Ik and Bhauein and Waterbend, the massive temple block of Jertin and the spiky columns of Sarantelku Ia, and then he reached a place where the buildings piled upon one another, an uneven mass of lumpy domes, and Last's voice fell silent.

Tolyat swallowed against the dryness in his throat. He should have brought something to drink; this work would take quite a while. And that was his mind, trying to distract itself from what it saw below.

"Chara e Pretyi," he said roughly, and wrote the name down with an unsteady hand.

Last cleared his throat. "Tolyat—"

He waved the man to silence. He didn't want to hear any reassurances Last might offer; he had left his home behind years ago, and he didn't regret the choice, however much the sight of it might pain his heart.

But Last spoke again, more urgently. "Tolyat!"

When he turned, Last flung one arm out, stabbing his finger through the air at something in the distance. Something *at their level* in the distance, flying toward them with speed.

How much speed was hard to judge. At first Tolyat thought it a bird, not too far away. Then the creature grew larger, and it was still not close. By the time he began to get a sense of its real size, Last was already thrashing among the equipment in the bottom of the basket. "Where in the name of all that's unholy did I put—"

Tolyat opened his mouth to ask what he was looking for, but the words turned into a sudden and delighted laugh. "Last, look!"

The creature was plummeting from the sky, the mad flapping of its wings doing no good whatsoever. Last, standing again, raked one hand through his black hair in a gesture of relief. "Wringe. Nothing that big can fly there. We're . . ." His hand stopped. "*Not* safe."

Because a host of other shapes had risen into the air, back in the direction the creature had come from. They flew more cautiously, but with a clear aura of purpose, and they wove back and forth in a way that said they knew which Shreds to avoid. They passed Wringe to either side and kept coming.

Last went back to digging and came up a moment later with a coiled thing like a whip made of jointed bone. He set his gaze on the nearest of the beasts, then snapped his arm outward. The whip uncoiled, and a burst of something starlike flew from the end to strike squarely in the chest of the creature.

Which didn't so much as miss a single wingbeat.

This time Tolyat was the one to dive into the pile, looking for anything of use. "What are they? And where do they come from?"

"Damned if I know!" Last growled above him. There was another fizzling crack of the whip, and a curse. "I told you, I don't know all of Driftwood; they aren't coming from anywhere in my territory. But this isn't working. We'd better drop, and fast." He turned to kneel, hands reaching for the nearest shauein stone, but before he could, Tolyat shot up again, clutching the furnace.

Last's black eyes went very wide. Laughter burst from him, and he took the furnace. "You realize this is crazy."

"I don't care," Tolyat said, and it was true. Last was right; they should drop back down, flee from the creatures, come back later with weapons that would do some good. But up here in the skies, he felt like the king of all Driftwood, and he was damned if he would let some beasties from another world chase him from his throne. "Will it work?"

Last grinned—a thing Tolyat had never seen before—and now the light in his eyes was pure madness. "Let's find out."

He whirled, pointing the furnace's mouth toward the nearest creature, who was now very close. The device was an oddly shaped thing; Tolyat would never have taken it for a furnace if Last hadn't called it by that name. Its squat, metal-sided body had no visible opening for fuel, only a projecting tube on one side that seemed to be an outlet. Last aimed this at the nearest beast, rotated the tube within its housing as far as it would go, and smacked the side with the heel of his hand.

An enormous gout of flame leapt out, leaving a stripe burned into Tolyat's vision. A discordant shriek raked his ears, and when he blinked the afterimage away, he saw the creature spiraling downward, trailing a cloud of smoke. Last shouted in triumph and aimed the furnace a second time.

But the creatures had already proved themselves intelligent. There were four of them left, and they ranged themselves apart, ducking and weaving to approach the basket from different angles. Up close, they were truly immense, with bright green feathers and snouts full of wicked teeth. Last released another jet of flame, which singed the rear left wing of one creature; it snarled and veered off its path, but did not fall.

Tolyat started hurling everything he thought he might not need. Measuring devices that had gone unused; they did no damage, but sometimes made the creatures dodge. Last shot a second one down, spitting curses in several different languages. Tolyat's pen case; it missed the beast he aimed at, but in its fall it struck another near the corner of its eye. Last spun to try and flame that one, and narrowly avoided lighting the basket on fire. Then Tolyat grabbed the ropes that attached the sack to the basket, intending to rip them free and fling the cloth over one of the creatures, like a net.

He fell before he could. Something slammed into the side of the basket, and then he wasn't the only thing falling: everything, basket and all, dropped with him.

His scream was torn away by the suddenly racing air. One of the creatures had knocked them off their axis, disrupting the connection between the shauein stones; the discs in the floor of the basket twisted, trying to maintain their orientation, and far below, the ones in the ground must be doing the same, but all it did was send the basket shooting off on a brief diagonal trajectory before it passed out of range. And then the fall began in earnest, with nothing more to stop it.

Tolyat heard Last screaming in his ear. "Up! Up!"

Of course *up*, that was the only solution to their current problem of *down*, but what in the name of every god was Tolyat supposed to do about it? Then he realized Last was shoving at him, trying to get at the fabric beneath his body. And Tolyat, on the principle that a slim chance was better than none, rolled clear and began to shove the sliding masses of fabric above his head.

As soon as he found the mouth of the sack, Last slammed the furnace down in the center of the basket and began drumming on its sides with all the desperation suitable to his life depending on it. Fire shot out again, but he must have done something to the furnace, because it wasn't the long jets of before; this was a smaller, steadier flame, though still hot enough to bake all the moisture from Tolyat's scales.

And the sack began to fill.

The wind of their fall did half the work, inflating the sack like the seed of a geschen tree. It perhaps slowed them a little bit, but not much; Tolyat, shoving the fabric up as if that would help make this crazy scheme work, saw the houses and ruins of Driftwood coming terrifyingly close. But still the furnace burned, and the air grew ever warmer—and then, in a form of magic Tolyat had never seen before, the basket began to float.

Last kept drumming, but more gently now, and after a few moments he stopped. With eerie grace, born aloft by a sack that now dwarfed the basket below, they drifted across the face of Driftwood.

It took few moments longer for Tolyat to believe he wasn't about to die. His legs no longer wanted to support him; he sank into a boneless heap, gasping. Last supported himself with arms draped along the basket's edge, his black eyes wide, but soon his expression came to life once more, and he began laughing.

Tolyat couldn't help but join him. It wasn't funny—it *shouldn't* be funny. They'd nearly died. Or at least *he* had; who knew what it would have done to Last. But in the aftermath, he felt more alive than he ever had.

Hauling himself up to his knees, Tolyat looked over the edge. They were much lower than before, low enough to see people in the streets and fields below, staring upward at the strange contraption floating overhead. Fields? They'd gone farther than he realized, out of the Shreds, into the Ring lands where there was still space to raise livestock and crops. He'd learned about such things—after all, he was a scholar—but never seen them with his own eyes. So this was where their food came from, bought for what little wealth the Shreds had left. The basket floated above the fields like a misshapen bird, riding the winds.

If they kept going, they might fly all the way to the Mist.

He turned and found his concern mirrored in Last's eyes. The guide fiddled with smaller strings dangling from the sack, and soon they began to drop, more gently than the precipitous speed of before. None too soon; they were nearing a world boundary, and the weather on the other side looked bad.

The basket came to rest in an open expanse of golden plants that looked very soft but poked uncomfortably through holes in the weave. Tolyat helped Last push at the sack as it deflated, so the fabric wouldn't collapse on their heads. Then, with reluctance, he climbed over the edge and stood on solid ground once more.

"Do you know where we are?" he asked.

Last jumped over the edge, with a lithe energy that belied what they had just gone through, and looked around speculatively. "Maybe? I think these are wheat fields, and if I'm right, I know who buys their grain. We'll get back home, don't worry."

Morosely, Tolyat reached into the basket and pulled out the fallen, trampled piece of paper that held his map. The lines were mostly clear, but unfinished. He hadn't done even a quarter of the work before they'd been chased from the sky.

From behind him came an incomprehensible word. "Achricks."

It sounded like a sneeze. "What?"

"Achricks," Last said. He nodded, a smile growing across his face. "Projectiles aren't a good idea—

they'd fall on the heads of innocent passersby—but achricks shoot energy, and I don't know of *anything* that can shrug them off. Though we should have a few other options, in case it's like the star-whip. My fault, really, for only bringing one weapon; I honestly didn't think anything in Driftwood could fly as high as you said we would go. Next time I'll be better prepared."

Tolyat's ruff lifted. "*Next time?*"

Last gestured toward the paper he held. "You aren't done, are you? I figure it will take at least a couple more trips, depending on how detailed you decide to be. Unless you've had enough?"

That weight, cast aside while they were in the sky, had started to settle upon him once more. Last's words stopped it. To go back. . . .

The man *had* to be immortal. There was no other explanation for why Last, having nearly died for Tolyat's mad dream, would be volunteering to do it again. Driftwood, for all its diversity, couldn't possibly hold *two* beings crazy enough to do this for fun.

"Do you have a knife?" Tolyat asked. While Last pulled one from his sleeve, Tolyat knelt and began looking for the edge of the mostly deflated sack. "I'll cut a piece to wrap the stones in, and you carry the furnace."

"Oh, so *now* you believe in magic floating hot air."

"Floating stones, floating hot air, anything that will keep me from falling out of the sky. Maybe we should find out where those beasts came from, see if it's possible to rent one as a bodyguard." His mind was full of plans. There was a woman in Candle-pot with a device that could make copies of things drawn on paper; he could sell the map when he was done. Or even sell trips to see Driftwood from above. What might it do, if people saw it with their own eyes?

He didn't know. What he did know was that he had his grand answer, and it was no less meaning-ful for being fun. The change in Last was enough to prove that.

With their most important equipment gathered, Last jerked his thumb toward a building just visible above the grain. "Let's get started. It's going to be a damn long walk back to the Shreds."

"Wait!"

Tolyat dove for the basket one final time. When he came up again, Last had his eyebrows raised. Tolyat flourished the pen he'd saved. "I want to take notes on the way back."

recorded by Yilime

The Outsider

THE MAP IS OLD, and it isn't even the original version. A copy of a copy of a copy, and Febrenew has two more stashed away somewhere else, in case he wakes up one morning to discover this latest specimen is what Driftwood has decided to take away. Even with those for insurance, this map is one of the first things he grabbed when the mud began to flood in from the mire above. The oldest version always hangs on the wall in Spit in the Crush's Eye. It's the closest thing to sacred that Febrenew has.

Dreceyl peers at it, squinting in the floating light that still bathes the amphitheater in its gentle glow. "I can't read any of this."

"None of us can," Febrenew says. "Chara e Pretyi is gone, and its language with it. All the places marked there are gone. Between you and me, I doubt any of the words would be readable even if Chara e Pretyi were still here; we've probably made mistakes while copying it. But that's not the point."

He rolls up the map as he speaks, tucking the beanbags into his pockets once more, and with Dreceyl's help slides it back into the cylindrical leather case. Then, to everyone's surprise, he begins to walk away, back to his makeshift bar, leaving the stage for others to claim.

"You aren't going to leave it on the memorial?" Ioi asks.

Febrenew stops and shrugs. "Why should I? Kuondae's a heartless thing, but I agree with her on one point. I don't think he's dead."

He holds up the map case, as if in explanation. Spread, its vaguely square shape is wider than he is tall, and he isn't short by any current standards. "Driftwood's a damn big place," he says. "And Last works in the Shreds more often than not—but not always. So what if we haven't seen him in a while? Could be he's just gone out to the Edge. Maybe for a job, or maybe just to get some time away. I *do* believe the stories about him—heard too much from my predecessors not to—and if I were him, I'd get tired of living among us, with the kinds of tales people tell about him. Making him out to be more than he is." He glares at the recorder at the front of the stands, who meets his gaze without blinking.

Then Febrenew turns his attention to everyone

else. "But here's the thing he'd want you all to remember. This place? It's your home. Not *this* place—" He stamps one foot against the cracked slates of the amphitheater's floor. "But Driftwood. The whole of it, more than any single bit, and the people in it as much as the ground we stand on. Those of us who are Drifters, anyway . . . but when you get down to it, all of us."

"Is that why he's survived?" Dreceyl asks. "Because he's made Driftwood his home, instead of any one bit of it?"

A twitch of the hand is Febrenew almost reaching out to ruffle the boy's hair, but the indignant hunching of Dreceyl's shoulders stops him. "I don't think so," Febrenew says, his tone kindly. "He's not the only one who feels that way about this place. And that doesn't stop old age from taking hold. But it's still a good thought, isn't it?"

His story and the words that followed have calmed the turmoil Kuondae stirred up. As Febrenew stows the map under his table and goes back to selling drinks and cheap noodles to the people at the memorial, another person takes the stage to relate their tale, how Last touched their life and made it better. Made Driftwood a little easier to bear. Like he was the thread stitching them together, against the constant unraveling of time.

Midnight has come and gone when the dark-skinned woman comes up and points at the pile of sweetpods. No one else is nearby, and as Febrenew cracks the fruit open and drains it into a cup, he says in a low voice, "You've been here from the start. Not just tonight, but ever since people began gathering. Either you're incredibly bored, you're in love with Last—or you're up to something. Want to tell me which one?"

The look on her face says that no, she does not. But after a hesitation, some internal argument is settled in favor of answering. "I'm neither bored nor in love. I'm worried. What you said about Last, that he might just have gone away for a time . . . I wish I could agree with you. But I'm afraid something truly has happened."

Febrenew braces his hands against the table, easing his aching feet, and incidentally leaning in closer so that others are less likely to overhear. "Are you the one who saw it? Whatever 'it' was."

She shakes her head. Here on the edge of the light, her expression is in shadow, and that's not always reliable across cultural boundaries anyway. People show different moods in different ways. "Not me. But . . . he said something to me, not long before he vanished."

"What?"

The woman hesitates. Febrenew sighs and says, "You haven't answered my question. You've been watching here for days, and 'I'm worried' doesn't tell me why. Whatever you're waiting for, it hasn't happened yet—and if you're waiting for Last himself to show up, I think you're going to be disappointed. He's never liked this kind of attention."

"I know," the woman murmured. "I didn't do this to bring him here. I was hoping . . ."

Her phrasing snags in Febrenew's mind. "Are you the one who started the memorial?"

The wreath of flowers from Aic, laid by an unknown hand. "Yes," the woman says. "Not as mourning, but as a prayer. Such things are the custom in my world, only the flowers we used are gone. As is the place where we once laid them. This was the closest approximation I could find. A place where no one lives."

One mystery answered—but not the biggest one. "Whatever you're hoping for, you're probably running out of time." Febrenew tips his head at the stage, where another speaker is taking up position. "This is nice, but I doubt you'll see the same thing tomorrow. People have lives outside of here. And the stories are giving them a feeling of resolution. After this they'll still wonder or mourn, but they probably won't come back."

She nods, sighing. It's a near-universal gesture, that deep exhalation, at least among all creatures that breathe air. "After this one is done, then. I don't want to interrupt."

Another customer approaches, and the woman goes to stand at the edge of the stage, waiting her turn. Febrenew glances up at the sky, trying to gauge how much longer they all have before self-preservation will require them to leave the amphitheater . . . but as his gaze comes back down, he sees shadows in the tunnel leading to the outside world.

And the hem of another robe, flickering briefly into the light.

He growls a curse in the deep register most Drifters can't hear or hit, inherited from a Zlanma great-grandparent. One robed idiot: that isn't a surprise, given the circumstances. But two . . .

The dark-skinned woman is taking the stage. Febrenew grits his teeth and waits.

Remembering Light

IN HER FIRST LIGHT, Noirin never thought it strange that her world should be only a few blocks square, and that on the other side of the Palace Way (whose palace had vanished before her grandmother was born) there should be a place where the people had four arms and water always fell from the sky. She never gave it any thought at all, until the day the chantry disappeared.

It stood—had stood—on the other side of Surnyao from the Palace Way, and at first dawn its long shadow had stretched across the intervening blocks, all the way to the boundary with Yimg, the place of rain. The Asurnya measured their world by that tower, the tallest they had left. Then one day the first sun rose and no shadow answered; the Asurnya looked to the sky and found it empty, and

Noirin realized what they meant by measuring the world, what her mother was talking about when she said there was once a sunset chantry on the other side of the Palace Way—that there had once been an "other side" that was not Yimg but Surnyao.

She grew up in the absence of that shadow, one absence among many. One more thing her people had lost. Noirin underwent the rites of early light in a ramshackle tower built to replace the missing chantry; by the time she reached her increasing light, that tower had collapsed. She departed her girlhood in a shabby building of only four stories, where the remaining suns could barely find her at all.

There were only two left. But Noirin faced the horizon anyway; she covered her eyes seven times, and whispered a sacred vow to the wind.

"I will recover what we have lost."

Surnyao, as it had been before the seventh sun burned out, and the end of the world began.

Before they came to Driftwood.

"You must not go," the Chant Leader said despairingly, when she told him of her intent. "I'm not a traditionalist, Noirin; you know I'm not. We once had the luxury of following the chants in the matter of travel, letting the suns dictate how far we went, but that was before the—" He choked on the words. "What you propose, though, is too much."

"In my increasing light," she answered him, inflecting her verbs with both respect and determination, "I am permitted to go out of the city of my birth. If that city has dwindled, it makes no difference; there is no reason I should not go."

Casuistry, and they both knew it. Before the end of the world, the chants had said that only those in their glorious light should go to the far ends of the earth. The traditionalist opinion, since Surnyao's arrival in Driftwood, held that to go *past* the ends of the earth was out of the question, even for such elders. But the world was a smaller place than it had been—much smaller, and ever shrinking—and tradition was, as the Chant Leader said, a luxury they could not afford. The fields that once fed them had withered and vanished, their mines crumbled into oblivion, and to survive, they were forced to trade with those beyond their borders. Those from other worlds.

Other worlds that were dying. Just like Surnyao.

Just before the seventh sun burned out, whole realms of Surnyao fell into Absent Light and were never seen again. But where they had been, instead there was a dark mist, and then something else in that mist: another land, foreign beyond comprehension, which had suffered its own disaster. Was still suffering. Flakes of fire whirled through the air there, and some of its people stood out in that wind until they burned to cinders, accepting—even welcoming—their demise. The rest dug into the ground for shelter, and traded with Surnyao and their neighbors through cramped tunnels that stank of ash.

That place was gone now. Noirin had never seen it. It had crumbled faster than Surnyao, slipping toward the center of Driftwood, into the Crush itself, from which nothing emerged again.

The Chant Leader would have buried his hands in his beard, but it had thinned with time, only a few black wires left. He had pulled the rest out, in his agony over the doom of their world. "We need you here, Noirin. You've memorized all the chants, every one we still remember—even the ones we no longer use. Who else cares as much as you? Who else can become Chant Leader, after I'm gone?"

She put her hand on his arm, felt it tremble beneath the thin silk of his robes. Worn, and much patched, but it was the last silk they had. "I'll come back. When I've found him."

"When!" he cried. "That was ages ago, Noirin. How many races in Driftwood live that long? Even if he lives, it will be like finding one spark of light in the blaze of seven suns."

Beneath that, the real protest: *if he ever lived at all.* The Chant Leader thought it a myth. But it was his job to remember everything, as much as he could, and so he told the story: the man who came to

Surnyao, who lived among the Asurnya for a time, and then went away. A man who might, if the stories were true, still live.

The Chant Leader dropped his face into his hands. "Noirin, the—" His voice caught again, and when he recovered, his whisper was low and intense. "The second sun will burn out soon."

It struck her with the chill of Absent Light. He could not know that for sure; it was a common pastime in Driftwood, trying to predict the decay of worlds, and equally common to mock those who tried. Would the first sun—the last one—come with them into the Crush, or would Surnyao go to that ultimate end in darkness? Either way, the loss of the suns was the best metric they had, and to lose one of the remaining two was a sign of how little time they had left.

How little time she had to find her quarry.

Noirin chose the strongest inflections she knew. "I will go out under the light of two suns," she said, "and return before the last burns out. I promise you, Chant Leader: I will come back. And I will bring hope with me."

But hunting through the Shreds was not so easy.

Here in the heart of Driftwood, nothing went very far. Not the worlds she walked through, small fragments like her own home, struggling to preserve themselves against the unstoppable decay. Not the oddments she brought with her, barter-pieces in an unpredictable economy where strange things could acquire value.

Even her determination faded faster than it should.

She expected her search to take a while. If the man she sought were nearby, she would have heard; Noirin therefore went to the edge of her range, the point at which people ceased to understand the pidgin she spoke. There she stopped for a time, taking a job in a Drifter bar, among people so crossbred they belonged to no world at all. She washed dishes with the juice of a plant whose original name was lost along with the world it came from, but which grew now in many parts of Driftwood and went by the humble name of rinseweed. While she worked, she learned a new trade-tongue, one used in Shreds more distant from her home. And then she moved on: all part of her plan.

What she hadn't planned for was loneliness.

Not for people—or at least, not only. She missed the two suns; too many Shreds had only one. She missed the chants, patched and ragged though they were. Those things had always kept her company before, and now their loss caught in her throat, so that she dwelt obsessively on her vow. *I will recover what we have lost.* It eroded her patience, as she found a new job, learned a new tongue, asked after the man she sought.

The sound of his name changed between languages, but the meaning did not. And he was a one-blood, not a crossbred Drifter; it made him distinctive. She found people who had heard of him, certainly—or at least heard the stories. But how to find him, where he lived . . . that, no one seemed to know.

One spark of light in the blaze of seven suns. How many people lived in Driftwood? She asked three scholars and got seven different answers; it depended on whether she meant just the Shreds, or also the Edge, the place where worlds arrived out of the Mist. But all seven numbers were high, and Noirin was seeking a single man.

She had terrible dreams of the second sun burning out. One Absent Light the dream was worse than it had ever been, and she jerked awake, wondering whether that was a sign. Whether her people now dwelt under the light of a single sun. Could she tell, this far beyond the edge of Surnyao? Worlds worked according to their own rules, and the Shred she was living in was nothing like her home. But some things a person could carry within herself.

She moved onward. Another Shred, another job, another tongue to learn. Her grasp of it was halting at best. She spoke it well enough, though, to understand a bird-winged man when he told her the most helpful thing she'd learned yet. "He doesn't like to be hunted," the creature said. "Hired, yes. Hunted, no."

Noirin thought this over while she chopped vegetables she didn't know the names of and threw them into a bin next to the bar's cook. Hired, not hunted.

Very well.

The third public house she worked in occupied the massive trunk of a tree in a Shred whose people had vanished before memory, leaving a forest that resisted the attempts of neighboring Shreds to cut it for wood. The tree had no doors—its bark flexed open to allow passage—so Noirin had to watch in all directions, but she had no difficulty spotting the man when he walked in.

And he spotted her just as easily. He stopped halfway in, growled something that sounded like a curse, and turned around.

"Wait," Noirin called, but he had already left.

She ran after him. He was easy to find, too tall to move quickly through the low branches, his skin silver-blue in the muted air. A branch snagged the loose fabric of his tunic, and it ripped with a sound like the rattle some Drifter musicians used. He swore again—then a third time, as Noirin caught up to him.

"Why did you run away?" she asked.

He glared at her. His eyes were as deep a black

as her own, oddly reassuring. "You're the one who's been hunting me."

What did she expect? She was a one-blood, as distinctive as he was among the Drifters; no one in this part of the Shreds had skin as dark as hers. She had moved to a new area before trying to hire him, but he was clever enough to make the connection on sight.

Noirin freed the torn edge of his tunic from the branch and wished any of the pidgins had the inflections of her native tongue; she couldn't express supplication well enough. "No. The rumor I spread was true; I want to hire you. To help my people."

He pulled away from her in disgust and fury. If the trees had let him, he likely would have walked away again, but there was no graceful exit to be had. "I can't save your gods-damned world."

A sound of startlement escaped her. "I didn't think you could."

Now she had his attention. He considered her, while he tucked the trailing flap of his tunic into his sash. "Then what did you want me for?"

Noirin wished they stood in sunlight, rather than the oppressive dark of the trees, but feared that asking him to move elsewhere would exhaust the small patience she'd won. "Are you the man known as Last?" The meaning stayed the same, no matter the tongue; she named him in the language of her home.

He went still at the sound of it; she could almost see the rapid dance of his thoughts, recognizing the language, trying to identify it. "Surnyao," he said at last, and a small sun of joy burned beneath Noirin's ribs. "The place of light."

"It used to be. And that is why I've searched you out."

"I can't put it back the way it was, either," he said, with a surprisingly bitter cast to the words.

She shook her head. Now was the time to ask; the bitterness wasn't directed at her. "Could we go somewhere . . . more comfortable?"

After a heartbeat, a grin broke through the twist of his face. "Either you're propositioning me, or you want sunlight."

Another startled sound. "No! You—you aren't—"

"Asurnya?"

"A *woman*," Noirin said. "At least you don't appear to be."

Understanding dawned in his eyes. "That's right; your people have rules about that sort of thing. So you're how old—third sun?"

Both the heat of embarrassment and the light of joy faded a little. "Nearly fourth," Noirin said. This time she was glad for the pidgin, so she didn't have to decide whether to inflect for shame or not. "Maybe fourth, by now; I'm not sure how long I've been gone."

"I'm not arrogant enough to think you'd hunt me

out for breeding, anyway. So you want sunlight, and to ask me about something else entirely." His next words were addressed to the trees. "All right, I'm listening to her. Will you let me go now?"

The branches, without seeming to move, opened up around them. Last grinned again at Noirin's wide eyes and said, "Little-known secret. The people of this Shred never vanished; it was only ever inhabited by trees. You've been waiting tables inside their king. Come on."

She absorbed that in wonderment, then stretched with relief as they came into the open air. The sun in this next Shred was weak, leaving her cold all the time, but it was better than nothing. Last led her between two buildings and into a courtyard she didn't know existed, where the ground gave way to a shallow bowl of beaten copper ten paces across. It caught the sun's weak light and gave back gentle warmth, and Noirin almost wept with sudden homesickness.

He gave her time to compose herself, then said, "So what *do* you want me for?"

At his nod, she seated herself gingerly on the copper, pressing her hands against the sun-heated metal. "We still have stories of you," she told him, faintly embarrassed to admit it. "They say you were in the place of fire, and the first outsider to set foot in Surnyao."

"Place of fire. . . ." His eyes went distant, and

then he snapped his fingers. "E Si Ge Tchi. I think. They were trying to negotiate a treaty with another world, for protection against that firestorm. Yes, I remember."

Radiant light, within and without. He remembered. Noirin said, "You are the only one who does."

"I thought you said your people told stories about it."

"About *you*. And a little about Surnyao, what it was like then. But the truth is that we've forgotten most of it. We talk about Absent Light and the vanished suns, but it's empty words, fragments without meaning. Nobody understands well enough to explain."

He turned his head away. She took the opportunity to study his profile: the folds of his eyelids, the sharp slope of his jaw, the copper light giving his skin a violet cast. So unlike an Asurnya man. And old—how old? He must come from a very long-lived race indeed, to have been there when Surnyao was new to Driftwood, and still be here now. But he had seen it with his own eyes, not filtered through generations of broken chants, memories warped by pain and loss.

Last said, almost too quiet for her to hear, "That's the nature of Driftwood. Fragments."

The pain in his voice made it hard for Noirin to speak. "And it's in the nature of those who come to Driftwood to fight against it. You *remember*. You can tell me how Surnyao was. And then I can go home, and tell my people, and we will take that light with us into the darkness."

It would come regardless. She knew that much. The last suns would burn out, and Surnyao would go into the Crush, as countless worlds had gone before them. But they could go as Asurnya, with the strength of all they had forgotten. They could make their own light.

He let out a breathless laugh. "Tell you? An entire world. Or most of one, anyway. I lived there for some time—no doubt your stories tell you that—from mid-sun to Absent Light. I could talk from now until your last sun dies and not tell you everything I saw, and you'd forget half of it before I was done."

She felt the pulse of her heart in her tongue. "You could come to Surnyao—"

He was on his feet before she saw him move, retreating to the center of the shallow copper bowl. "And see the wreckage of a place I once loved? No. I won't be your new Chant Leader, won't bind myself to—"

And then he stopped, before Noirin could find a response, and in the warm glow she saw speculation dawn on his face. "Though perhaps," he said, and stopped again.

She dug her fingers into the unyielding copper. "What?"

He hesitated for a moment, then said, "You'd have to do something for me in return."

"I always intended to," she said. "Nothing in Driftwood is free. What do you want?"

Last said, "To forget."

The sign above the archway was unintelligible to Noirin, but Last told her it read *Quinendeniua*. The Court of Memory.

Walls of packed and polished mud surrounded the courtyard, and fragrant trees bloomed along the walls, breathing forth their scent in the light of flickering torches. In one corner, a creature of amorphous shadow served drinks to patrons, and in another, four musicians provided a melody to the dancers who swayed across the paving-stones.

And that was all. Quinendeniua was the only remnant of its world; beyond its earthen walls, other Shreds went about their business. But the sound did not carry across the threshold, as if this were a sacred space.

Last felt it, too, for he spoke in a quiet tone that went no farther than Noirin's ears. "There are two ways to do this. But if you chased me down to find the memory of Surnyao's past, I doubt you want to begin with blasphemy. You haven't been presented to the fourth sun yet."

In the warm darkness, she could scarcely feel the heating of her own cheeks, and she managed a light response. "Even if I were—you're not arrogant enough to expect that."

His teeth glinted silver when he grinned. "Right. Well, for this to work, we have to match each other; we have to move as one. So, like most people who come here, we dance."

"Are—" She stared at the figures moving in the torchlight. "Are they all here for memory?"

"One way or another. It's the magic of this place. Some people want to remember someone else's memories—for education, or just for escape. Others want to forget. Memories can be shared, or given away." His eyes vanished into the darkness beneath his brows when he looked down at her. "How do you want to begin?"

The memory he wished to lose was not Surnyao; he'd refused to tell her what it was. What could be so bad that this man would want to erase it from his mind? It was at least partly morbid curiosity that made Noirin say, "My payment is that you will forget. Let that be done first."

"So I don't have to worry you'll skip out on the bill," he said, and managed a hint of amusement. "I appreciate it. But no—I'll give you what you came for, first."

His fingers curled around hers, and he pulled her forward before she could protest.

The music was foreign but lovely, a slow beat from skin-covered drums and some kind of rattle, stringed instruments like leudani weaving melody and harmony around it. Noirin could not understand the singer's words, but the sense of them reached her anyway: memory and forgetfulness, the foundations and chains of the past. She didn't know whether the connection of minds came about through the music, or if Quinendeniua did it to all who came within, but she believed what Last had told her was true.

Here, she could see what he had seen, more completely than words could ever convey.

Here, she would remember Surnyao.

The dances of her home were long forgotten. She had seen others in her travels, some frantic, some like the slow movement of statues. This was neither. *We have to move as one*, Last had said; he drew her close, wrapped one arm about her waist. They were closer in height than she had thought, and could lay their heads upon each other's shoulders. She felt the tremor of his laughter. "I know it's strange. Just relax. In a moment, you won't notice this at all."

She wasn't sure she believed him. But he began to move, in slow, easy steps, and she moved with them; she couldn't *not*, as close as they were. His free hand held hers lightly, like a bird. Despite the darkness, the air was warm, and a pleasant sweat beaded her skin. Noirin closed her eyes, gave Last her trust, felt him give the same to her. There was nothing but the darkness and the music, the scented breeze, the firmness of the paving-stones beneath their feet, and memory. . . .

Seven suns, blazing their glory across the sky, a brightness and a heat that gave life to everything below.

Chants, *always* chants, not just at certain times but continually, their steady pace the means by which the Asurnya measured their days. *I will meet you at the Hyacinth Canto. You haven't come to see me in a hundred cycles. Fry the meat for one stanza.*

Tall towers that cast no shadow, lit from every side by the suns. In the catacombs beneath them, warriors with spears of black iron, the priesthood of Absent Light. Figures of terror, to small children—*behave, or I'll apprentice you to the Harbingers of the Dark.*

Markets that sold a thousand spices, each one distinct on the tongue. Aromatic flowers that danced in the gentle air, their seeds spreading in the ceaseless light. Serpents dozing in the warmth, sold as pets, as sacrifices, as food. Vast fields, kept damp by intricate irrigation, regulated by a caste called the saerapavas.

A young man. Tall and slender, black as obsidian, with a merry grin. In his third sun, he was too young for breeding, and so he dallied with his male friends until that time came. Even with a silver-pale outsider, horrifying the Chant Leader, who insisted that contact with someone from beyond the edges of the world would be an abomination, regardless of age.

Last loved Chahaya, and mourned when he reached his median light, moving into the world of women and family.

Grief threatened to suffocate Noirin—hers and Last's. *This* was the world they had lost, in all of its wondrous complexity, from the heartbreaking perfection of the ancient chants to the shameful poverty of the beggars in the streets. Good and bad, grand and humble, all the different aspects of Surnyao, and the suns watching it all in their slow march across the sky.

Absent Light.

Wails throughout the city, the terrified shrieks of children. She could not feel the terror herself: to Last, it was simply night, a common enough occurrence in most worlds. And now it came too often for her to comprehend its full horror. But she witnessed the paralysis of the Asurnya, the Harbingers walking the streets with their black iron spears, and heard the silence where the chants had been.

Then dawn, the First Sun, blessing the world with its light.

And Surnyao came to life once more.

The shoulder of Last's shirt was wet with tears when Noirin lifted her head.

"I'm sorry," she said, and tried ineffectually to brush it dry.

He stopped her with one hand. "It's all right." Grief shadowed his eyes, too; he had remembered Surnyao with her. So much lost! She thanked light he'd left when he did; she did not want to remember the moment after his departure, when the Glorious Sun burned to cinders on the horizon. That horror lived on well enough in tales.

He let her pull free. Noirin retreated out of the way of their fellow dancers, going to stand beneath one of the trees. Tiny pink petals drifted down, reminding her of similar trees that had once bloomed in the gardens of the chantries.

When she had composed herself once more, she turned and found Last waiting at a discreet distance. Torchlight flickered behind his head, but his face was in shadow. "What do you want to forget?" she asked him. "What is so terrible, the very memory of it must be torn from your mind?"

He didn't answer at first. This was not part of their agreement, that she should ask questions. But finally he said, "Not terrible. Just—" A ragged breath, and for the first time it occurred to her that he might have chosen his position deliberately, to hide his expression in darkness. She understood him better now, and she knew the ways in which honesty was hard for this man.

"Just painful," he finished.

Noirin left him his distance, but not his reticence. "You bear so much grief. Why is this pain worse than all the others? Last . . . what are you trying to forget?"

And she knew, fleetingly, as she said it, that she had used the wrong name; he was not always called Last. But she didn't know what his real name was.

He answered her anyway. "My world."

The weight of it was there, in her memory. Rarely at the forefront of his mind, but always present. He was old, far older than she had realized; old when Surnyao came to Driftwood, and far older than he should ever have been.

Last of his race. Last of his world, which had long since gone into the Crush. Living on, with no idea why, ages after he should have been dead. And something had happened to him, a recent pain, which made him want to forget where he had come from, forget there was one world he would grieve for beyond all others, now and forever, with no end in sight.

She didn't know what that recent pain was, how it had driven him to this desperate point. But she knew why he'd chosen to share Surnyao with her first: to postpone the moment when he would give up the memory of his own home. And she could guess the reason for that, too.

"You're the only one who remembers," Noirin said. His world, and countless others that had come and gone. "If you forget . . . then they're dead, even if you live."

"Maybe I want that," he said harshly, cutting across the steady rise and fall of the music.

"For now. But not forever. There will come a time when you regret the loss of those memories. And who will remember them for you then?"

Last dropped his chin. Staring at the paving stones, he said, "This is not what we agreed."

No, it wasn't. And Noirin could not deny the curiosity burning within her. To know the origin of this man—his name, the name of his world, the path that had led to his immortality, even if he didn't understand it himself. She would know what he knew, what no one else in Driftwood did.

But she would be stealing his very self from him. If he forgot those things, he wouldn't be Last anymore. It was a form of suicide.

She had agreed. Noirin struggled with her conscience, then snatched at the hope of compromise. "If we do this . . . that memory becomes mine, in its entirety."

"Yes."

"Then I could keep it for you. And when you ask, we'll come back here, and I'll return it to you."

His head came up in a swift arc. Small shifts in his posture told Noirin he almost spoke several times, pulling the words back just before they reached his lips. Finally a broken half-laugh escaped him, and he said, "I should have known better than to think Quinendeniua would be so simple. Letting you in my head like that . . . you understand me too well now, don't you?"

She had no idea what he meant by that, but kept her silence.

"You could walk out that archway and be mugged in the streets of Vaiciai, or a dozen other Shreds between here and your home. You could die of old age or disease before I come find you. We could return and find Quinendeniua gone, just a crumbled chunk of wall dissolving in the Crush, and no world left that can do what this place does. A hundred and one ways for that memory to be lost. And without it. . . ."

Another long pause. This time, Noirin completed the sentence for him, because he'd said enough that she did indeed understand him now. "Without it, you might die."

"I don't know why I haven't," he said. "For all I know, forgetting might make it happen."

"Then the question is: are you prepared to destroy the last piece of your world?"

She didn't want to ask it. If he said yes, then she would have to do as she promised, taking his memory, destroying him in spirit, and maybe in body, too. But that was his choice, not hers.

Last buried his head in his hands, while behind him the dancers swayed and whirled, trading memories, remembering and forgetting events, people, worlds.

He lowered his hands. "No. I don't want to forget."

Noirin let out the breath she hadn't realized she was holding. Giving Last space for privacy, she went past him to the bar, paid for a drink with the ingots of iron that were her wages in the sentient tree where she had waited tables, what felt like a world's lifetime ago. Surnyao had no iron anymore, no Harbingers of the Dark. She pushed the memory aside and returned to Last with the cup.

He downed its contents, unconcerned with the possibility that the drink of this world might be poison to him. Then again, could anything harm him? She hadn't seen enough to know.

"Thank you," she said, and not just on behalf of Surnyao.

Last grunted. Then he seemed to reconsider that answer, staring at his empty cup, and said, "It'll pass. I've wanted to forget before—but this is the first time I've had a way to follow through. I think . . . I think I'll be glad when Quinendeniua is gone."

And with it, the temptation of oblivion. Noirin understood.

He set the cup aside and said, "I'll guide you back

to Surnyao. There's some bad Shreds between here and there."

Side by side, not quite touching, they passed under the arch of Quinendeniua, leaving behind the dancers and the music, the falling petals of the trees. Seven suns burned in Noirin's mind, lighting the way home.

recorded by Yilime

The Believer

B Y THE TIME she finishes, Noirin is weeping. Not ostentatiously; her voice remains strong and her posture straight. But tears slip down her face, and they glint gold in the soft light from above.

"That was . . ." She hesitates, wrestling with the ever-present difficulty of how to describe time in Driftwood. "Almost thirty Absent Lights ago. Our nights, though even now, those do not come as often for us as they do for other worlds. Recently. Enough so that I fear the mood which held him when we parted. He chose not to forget, but . . ." Noirin draws in a slow, steadying breath. "But that doesn't mean something else hasn't happened. That—that he hasn't done something else."

She folds her hands tight around each other and

scans the tiers of the amphitheater. They're nearly full now—full as they likely haven't been since the end of the world that used to contain them. It's still black night, but dawn can't be too far off; for their safety, the gathered mourners and gawkers will soon have to leave. But no one seems eager to move.

"I placed the wreath of flowers here," Noirin says, "not only for Last, but in order to draw people to this place. To see if anyone would come forward and claim they were the one who saw it. The story came to Surnyao that Last was seen walking into the Crush . . . but I know what rumor is like. It changes things. Makes them up, even. Perhaps someone just wanted to hurt us all, to make us think the one constant presence in Driftwood was finally gone.

"But no one has stepped forward. If I can't find the witness, then I'm going to believe that it's a lie: that Last has simply gone elsewhere, perhaps for a job, perhaps to get away for a time. And I am going to search for him, because he helped me and I'm worried for him.

"If that person is here, though . . ."

Noirin's voice grows ragged, and she stops. The silence in the amphitheater is absolute. Even sound from the neighboring Shreds seems not to pierce the tension.

And then a woman says, "I am here."

She steps out from the tunnel that gives access to the amphitheater, and she is not alone. Behind her are nearly a score of others, spilling like water from the archway, pooling behind the woman with their hands slipped inside their sleeves.

Every one of them wears a pale, silvery-blue robe. The same color as the recorder's robe. The color of Last's skin.

Febrenew's breath hisses between his teeth. Not just two; many. And when they turn out in force like this, it means they're planning something.

The silence of the amphitheater breaks into a rising growl, spiked with a few half-shouted accusations and declarations of unwelcome. Half-shouted only, because a lot depends on exactly which group has come to join the memorial. Like everything else in Driftwood, a movement can splinter, and not everything remains as it originally began. Those robes can hide quite a few things, and in some cases those things have turned out to be weapons.

The woman at the front of the group pushes back her silver-blue hood, revealing hair dyed solid black and a sharp face lit by inner fire. To those who seek a justification for disavowing her, Teryx isn't a true Drifter; her mother was Xerl and Hawblin, her father a one-blood from Neraful. But she calls none of those worlds her home: instead she travels through the Shreds, mastering every pidgin she encounters, so she can gather more people to her fold.

Of all those who could have come, she is not the worst. But she is also far from the best.

Surnyao is too far from the heart of the Shreds, and Noirin's search for Last caught only some of the stories about him. She doesn't recognize the significance of the robes, the hair. "Who are you?"

Teryx smiles, as if she's been waiting for someone to ask. "I am the only one in all of Driftwood who truly understands Last. Not simply as a guide, nor even as a man who chances to be immortal—the *truth* of Last. And I have come to tell you all what has happened to him."

"You saw him walk into the Crush?"

Teryx gestures for her people to stay where they are and begins to approach Noirin. Febrenew is out from behind his table before he realizes he's moving, and Teryx smiles with unsettling sweetness at him. "I know I am not welcome in your bar . . . but this is not your bar."

For the first time, the recorder who has been watching the proceedings speaks up. "You should have more respect. One of your predecessors counted herself among our number. And while you may not share her beliefs, you still make copies of that map."

That stops Febrenew in his tracks. Even the best efforts to preserve traditions still lose bits and pieces along the way—like the origins of the third promise made by every owner of Spit in the Crush's Eye. He knows why Last and Tolyat made the map, but not why generations of people have gone to such lengths to preserve it.

Noirin makes a little gesture, the same gesture Teryx made a moment before. She wants answers; someone has come to offer them. Noirin doesn't want Febrenew interfering. Gritting his teeth, he retreats and lets Teryx take the stage.

She kneels for a moment in front of the memorial and lays one hand on the nearest tribute, a small wooden carving of some six-legged animal. Her nails are dark, stained with some liquid that's growing out slightly at the cuticle. She says a few words in some language Noirin doesn't recognize—not one of the Shreds pidgins. It has the sound of a prayer, but not of mourning.

More like triumph.

Out of politeness, Noirin waits until Teryx rises, but then she can hold herself back no longer. "I asked you a question. You saw this? With your own eyes?"

Teryx smiles again, an unsettlingly peaceful expression. "With my own eyes, yes. I dare go closer to the Crush than anyone save Last himself, because I have no fear. Because I have faith."

She spreads her dark-nailed hands wide and says in a ringing voice, "Let me tell you of the god of Driftwood."

The God of Driftwood

THE CHILDREN had a game they played. They called it a game, even though it wasn't very fun; it was more of a challenge. A dare. A way for the bolder ones to frighten the more timid, to taunt the ones who refused. *Weakling. Coward. Dust.*

The adults, when they bothered to notice, said it wasn't weakness or cowardice not to play. It was common bloody sense. But that didn't carry much weight with children. And so Ctarl had been to the edge of the Crush again and again, trying to make his feet carry him just a step farther, just two, just as far as that one-legged fragment of arch that stood, improbably, after the rest of it was gone—if it could manage that much, against the twin forces of gravity and Driftwood, then surely he could manage to walk a few paces more and touch the arch before he ran away.

He never could. And Fanix mocked him for it every time. Then Ctarl would go home to his father, who found different kinds of fault with him. Ctarl had tried to tell his father once about the game, and got a beating for it. He still wasn't sure whether the beating was because he was stupid enough to play the game, or because he was too afraid to go closer. Or both.

It didn't really matter. Ctarl's father would always find a reason, no matter how hard Ctarl tried to be good, to please his father, to avoid things that might set him off. Life with him was like life in Driftwood: the things you relied on might crumble between one day and the next, and some new problem would rear its head. Ctarl was used to it. Ctarl told himself he was used to it.

Until the day things got bad enough that he ran: away from his father, toward the Crush, and he didn't stop where he always froze, didn't even stop at the one-legged arch.

Because there were things worse than the Crush. Worse than the place where the final remnants of every world died. What was there to fear in death? Death was just an end, and ends were good. They might hurt you, but then they *stopped*. And that was better than Ctarl's father.

He couldn't run very far, but only because the

way got too narrow and cramped for him to move quickly. Then there wasn't even a way—just gaps between the bits and pieces. He climbed over a fallen pillar, squeezed through a crack in a collapsing wall, stumbled across a patch of hip-high plants blooming with brilliant pink flowers, fell into a pool of salty water no more than two paces across but deeper than his eyes could see. He'd completely lost his bearings, but he kept looking for wherever the tangle was thickest, wherever things seemed the most broken. Because that would take him farther into the Crush, until he reached the place where he, like everything in Driftwood, would die.

The world swam in Ctarl's vision, tears or disintegration or both, and his pulse came loud in his ears. Every part of him ached—maybe the Crush was stealing him away already, a tendon here, an organ there. He sobbed so hard he could barely breathe, and then he slammed into something and fell and he really *couldn't* breathe. They called it the Crush, and he could feel its weight, crushing the life out of him.

But ends were good. They hurt you, but then they stopped.

The pain stopped. From a very great distance Ctarl heard a voice say, "Come on. You'll be all right."

He woke in a bed.

He was wrapped in an old shirt and he hurt all over. But he was clean, and someone had bandaged the worst of his injuries—both the ones his father had given him, and the ones he'd taken in his headlong flight.

He didn't understand.

Ctarl lay curled on the mattress, which felt like it was stuffed with something nicer than straw, and tried to look around the room without moving anything more than his eyes. People told stories about what waited on the other side of the Crush, but most of those stories belonged to worlds and the one-bloods who belonged to them. People interpreted Driftwood according to their own religions, their own beliefs. Drifters like Ctarl didn't have a world of their own, just the Shreds they lived in. They mostly said that what lay on the other side of the Crush was nothing at all.

This wasn't nothing. The bed was narrow, but soft; the curtain dangling from the ceiling was the kind of patchwork he was used to seeing around the Shreds, but much more carefully stitched. Faint light came through where the fabric was thinner or paler. The ceiling above him looked strangely furry, and he stared at it for a long, terrified moment, but he didn't see it breathe or shift, so he hoped it wasn't alive.

He wondered whose afterlife he'd ended up in.

A soft humming made him close his eyes. A moment later the light brightened against his eyelids; someone had drawn aside the curtain. Cooler air brushed his face. Then darkness and warmth, and faint sounds and the scent of onions: someone was bending over him. He stayed rigid as they pulled the blanket aside. But when hands touched the shirt over his ribs, he couldn't hold still any longer.

Ctarl yelped and pulled away so hard he smacked his head into the wall. The figure was a menacing shadow, its face invisible, its hands outstretched—but then it backed away and lowered itself carefully to the floor, speaking in a pidgin he barely understood, something about calm and hurt.

The voice was deep, but the body was soft and rounded, the face almost girlish. But wrinkled girlish, and the person moved like they were elderly, with effort and care. Their clothing showed the same neat stitching as the curtain, and some of the same fabric.

They went on, in a tone Ctarl thought was probably meant to be soothing and almost worked. More things about hurt, and drink, and sleep, and then something he didn't understand at all. The stranger saw his confusion then, and mimed flailing. It made Ctarl flinch back, and they stopped. Then he caught another word he recognized: *healing.*

That was something living people did. "I'm not . . ." Ctarl said, then stopped.

He'd spoken in the pidgin he was used to using, and the stranger frowned. Haltingly, they said, "You speak . . . this . . . yes?"

Wordlessly, Ctarl nodded.

"I Tinaamy," the stranger said. "In house I find you. Me house. Bad hurt. I help. Not easy—you die almost."

Memory pressed down on him, like the force of the Crush. "I was trying to die," Ctarl whispered.

Tinaamy's girlish face collapsed into an expression of warmth and pity. "Oh, child," they said, their voice deep and gentle. "Someone saved you."

Ctarl got the story later, once he spoke Tinaamy's pidgin well enough to understand it. They'd come home to find Ctarl just inside their front door—a door that was supposed to be locked, and still was—along with a basket of starfruit from Barkstep, which for Tinaamy's body was food enough for several months. Working outward from the places both of them knew, Ctarl and Tinaamy realized he was across the Crush from where his father lived, and Tinaamy offered to help him get home.

Ctarl refused violently enough that Tinaamy never mentioned it again. And they never asked why he'd run into the Crush, but he suspected they knew.

A story full of holes. How had Ctarl gotten out of the Crush, and inside Tinaamy's home? Who left the starfruit? Tinaamy said they had no idea, but Ctarl knew.

He'd been saved by the god of Driftwood.

Who else—*what* else—could possibly be waiting inside the Crush? Normal people were terrified of it. Even the children playing their game never went anywhere as deep as Ctarl had gone. The only people who did that were trying to die. And Ctarl doubted that a fellow would-be suicide had rescued him.

No, Driftwood had a god. One who lived inside the Crush, who took pity on him because it wasn't his time to go.

"You're not the first to think of that," Tinaamy said. "All the worlds that come here, they have gods—most of them, anyway—but others have decided that Driftwood must have a god of its own. A friend once told me about them. The ideas people have had before."

Ctarl sat up, interest sharpening. "What did those people say?"

Tinaamy shrugged, paying more attention to the leaves they were methodically grinding than to Ctarl and his excitement. "They usually think it's a malicious god. Eating worlds because it's forever starving. They never talk about it showing *pity*." They tossed in another handful of leaves and prodded the mass with the pestle as if it might speak.

"But nobody's ever found proof of its existence, either—except that Driftwood itself exists."

"Nobody except for me," Ctarl said.

They argued about it a lot as Ctarl grew up, because at first Tinaamy insisted he stay until he was healed, and then by the time he felt well they'd fallen into a comfortable enough routine that Tinaamy never hinted he should leave. Ctarl learned more languages, helping Tinaamy with patients, because they were a healer with the ability to make sure wounds stayed clean and never festered. Ctarl thought it was magic; Tinaamy insisted it was just skill; the word didn't really matter. It had kept Ctarl from dying: the power of Tinaamy's hands, and the mercy of the god of Driftwood.

A god Tinaamy didn't believe in. But that was all right. They hadn't seen what he'd seen.

He got a reputation as an eccentric. Ctarl didn't hesitate to tell people what had happened to him, and every day he went to the fringes of the Crush and thanked the god inside for helping him. He brought offerings, too: little things mostly, because he'd come out with nothing except his ruined clothes, and Tinaamy was too good-hearted to charge their patients even a quarter of what they should. But if people were right and the god of Driftwood was always hungry, maybe feeding Him voluntarily was good, rather than waiting for things to slide gradually into His maw.

So it went, as Ctarl grew from a boy into a youth, and then to the edge of manhood. And then Unokucatuin found him.

Ctarl was a Drifter through and through, and didn't really give a shit what sorts of long and complicated names Edgers and one-bloods clung to. Unokucatuin told him again and again that abbreviating someone's name was a sexual proposition in his world, but Ctarl found "Unokucatuin" too long and unwieldy to say all the time, so finally he offered the man a new name entirely: Oruc.

"But you have to earn it," Ctarl said. "Submit yourself to the god of Driftwood, and receive His mercy. Then you will earn a new name."

"You took the name Ctarl after you came out?" Unokucatuin asked, a little suspicious.

"Yes," Ctarl said, because there was nobody to really dispute it. He'd never gone back to where his father lived, and by now the man might be dead. Even if Tinaamy realized he'd always been called Ctarl, they wouldn't say anything. It was a just a maneuver so Ctarl wouldn't have to say "Unokucatuin" all the time.

But the part about sending the man into the Crush was real. Unokucatuin was from a world just now moving into the Ring, far enough from the Edge and shrinking small enough that his people were beginning to really panic about the inevitability of Driftwood. He'd heard about Ctarl from a Shreds merchant who traded out there, gas-driven devices from Lupyaconwi in exchange for grain, and he figured that it only made sense to learn about the god of this place and how to propitiate Him.

It was the first time anyone had treated Ctarl as anything other than a young man with an eccentric quirk. But if someone else wanted to worship the god of Driftwood, then it only made sense that they should follow the same path he had.

"Go in as deep as you can," he told Unokucatuin—it would be such a relief when he could call the man Oruc instead. "Surrender yourself completely to His mercy. You must be prepared to die, and not shrink from it." There was no point in trying to re-create his specific route; Ctarl couldn't remember most of it, and it would have crumbled by now anyway. Two entire Shreds had been abandoned to the Crush since his own rescue, their inhabitants too afraid to live so close.

Unokucatuin kissed him, which in his world was a gesture of deep respect and *not* a sexual advance. "I will," he said fervently. "There is nothing I would not do for my people."

He meant it. The next day he purified himself according to a ritual Ctarl made up for him because Unokucatuin seemed to expect something of that kind, and then he walked, without a hint of fear, into the Crush.

Ctarl waited all that day and through the night, and through the next day as well. He didn't know how long he'd been inside himself, before the god brought him out, and he was waiting with quick-beating heart for the chance to see his god again. But when no one appeared, it occurred to him that Unokucatuin—Oruc, now—might have been taken somewhere else to recover, as he had been. And so, reluctantly, Ctarl abandoned his post to search all around for a man fitting that description.

He found nothing. Dizzy with horror and lack of sleep, Ctarl went back to the Crush and stared into its depths.

He'd found a disciple—and promptly sent the man to his death.

Things seemed to vanish while he watched, a few bricks off the top of a wall here, a paving stone there. This was why people didn't look at the Crush; they didn't want to watch the process of Driftwood happening before their very eyes, lest they be the thing to vanish next. Even Drifters were superstitious about things like that.

Drifters.

In a flash that felt like his spirit coming unmoored from his body, Ctarl understood.

There was a god of Driftwood, yes—but He was not a god for one-bloods like Unokucatuin. He was for people without gods of their own, people without worlds of their own, people for whom Driftwood *was* their world. Tinaamy had mentioned it once, as a thing others had said in the past, but Ctarl had forgotten.

The god of Driftwood was the god of Drifters. Only for them would He show His power.

Ctarl bowed low, then fumbled in his pockets for an offering. He came up with a string of beads used as trade currency in a good third of the Shreds, and without hesitation flung it as far into the Crush as he could.

"I understand," he told his god, breathless with epiphany. "And now I know what to do."

It helped that no one knew about Unokucatuin. Ctarl might have had a difficult time convincing anyone else to listen to him if they knew the first man who'd done so had died.

But he was sure of his new revelation. And in time, he proved he was *right*.

Before, Ctarl had just been an eccentric. After Unokucatuin vanished—he made a point now of always using the man's full name, not just calling him "Uno" or "Oruc," even if it was only in his head—Ctarl became a priest. Instead of just making offerings, he carried his message to the people of the Shreds, his fellow Drifters and the chosen of his god.

Most of them laughed him out of the room. But not all.

His second disciple was a woman named Madzizi whose ancestry traced to at least a dozen worlds. She had just lost her beloved twin sister and felt the pain of the loss as acutely as Ctarl had felt his own. Madzizi walked into the Crush ready to die, and walked out again a little while later with her face serene. Ctarl was ever so faintly disappointed; he'd still hoped to see his god with his own eyes, when He brought Madzizi out. But it was enough for Ctarl to know that he was right: the god blessed Drifters, not one-bloods.

He didn't tell Madzizi to change her name. There wasn't any need for that, and maybe he'd been wrong to have that idea in the first place.

Ctarl wondered a lot about the variables. Did the timing matter? Direction of approach? Age? Madzizi was about the age Ctarl was now, years after his own salvation; Unokucatuin had been older. Or maybe it was the pain in the heart that their god responded to, and those who weren't ready to die from grief or despair wouldn't be saved. He tried to discourage the next disciple from going in, because Netaxhais was more or less contented with her life. When he found Madzizi waiting for her near the Crush, he realized they'd disobeyed him, and he feared the worst. But Netaxhais came out laughing and smiling, hugging Madzizi in thanks, and he realized their god's mercy was not only for those who suffered the most.

Even then, it didn't always work. For every ten that went in, one might not emerge again. The risk kept their numbers small, especially since Ctarl couldn't demonstrate any kind of powers granted to him or his disciples by their god. A few of them had abilities inherited from one lineage or another, but they performed no new miracles, developed no talents unique to themselves and separate from the worlds they lived in.

Ctarl didn't mind. For him, it was enough to have been saved. But it made it harder to convince others to join him in his faith.

By then Ctarl had stopped living with Tinaamy. The rooms they previously lived in had collapsed into a sinkhole, and the new place they'd found wasn't large enough for two adults. Tinaamy didn't like what he was doing anyway. "I've respected your belief in this god," they said, "even if I think you're wrong. Some passerby saw you go in and braved the risk in order to save you. If it pleases you to think otherwise, so be it. But encouraging others to join you—that's dangerous. How many of them have died?"

Only a few, and he kept looking for ways to improve their chances. Tinaamy themself had more than once performed dangerous procedures on patients; sometimes the patient died. They didn't see it as the same kind of thing, though, no matter how much Ctarl argued.

So it was easier for Ctarl to find a ramshackle structure built mostly out of cloth stretched between supports, and to move in there with as many of his disciples as could join him. They worked at a variety of jobs to support their priest and spread the word of their faith wherever they went, while Ctarl and Madzizi conducted the rituals Madzizi helped him develop.

She was good at rituals—better than Ctarl was. Good at seeing the meaning in things, and finding ways to share that meaning with everyone else. The Shred they lived in had lost even its name, but it still had a sun, and every morning when it rose Ctarl and Madzizi went to a small crag that overlooked the Crush, the last remnant of some long-decayed mountain range. From its top they spoke their prayers and made their offerings, using a device Netaxhais had found in Anutsrihc to send each object through the air in a long, graceful arc to land somewhere amid the uninhabited debris. For these ceremonies Ctarl wore a patchwork robe, deliberately stitched together out of many different fragments of cloth; each disciple that joined him contributed a piece. That was another of Madzizi's ideas.

They helped each other. Deep in the Shreds,

community could be as fragmented as anything else; Ctarl had grown up among people who had to fight for the necessities of survival, food, water, shelter, all the while knowing that tomorrow the column that held up the awning might be gone, or the spring in what was left of Uiriquin might run dry and leave them hiking all the way to Petal for water. By preference they fought people farther out, because those people had more to take, but the desperate sometimes turned on each other, too.

Not his faithful. If someone was in need, the others didn't hesitate to help. "We *are* Driftwood," Ctarl said in one of his early sermons. "Our ancestors came from a hundred different worlds, but they all became part of Driftwood in the end. We are the whole, built from a hundred different pieces. Separately we die; together we endure."

It became their motto, their mantra. *We are Driftwood. Separately we die; together we endure.*

On the surface, everything was good. Ctarl might not have a great many converts, but those he had were fervent, and surely their worship was pleasing to their nameless god. Except that Ctarl received no reply—and when his followers clamored for one, he found himself looking for small ways to satisfy them, reading omens into small coincidences here and there.

Was he relying on a true spiritual insight? Or deceiving the faithful so they wouldn't abandon him?

Madzizi was the best, and the worst. She more than anyone kept pressing Ctarl for more: now that they had a small community, what did their god want them to do? What was their purpose? She was looking for Ctarl to lead them somewhere, he realized—but if he was meant to do so, he'd missed the signs. Doubt began to dig its fingers in.

Then, as before, his path changed. It began with a man, and it ended with a death.

He should have taken a new name.

It might not have helped. He'd inherited his father's double-spotted eyes, two pupils in each iris. Some of his followers had taken that as a mark of divine favor, even though he'd told them it was simply a rare trait, found among a people who were all but gone now. So far as Ctarl knew, in fact, only one full-blooded Mtoe remained alive—and when that man heard of a Drifter with double-spotted eyes leading a "cult" on the other side of the Shreds, he came looking.

Rtean caught his son just after the morning devotions were done, climbing down the last stretch of the crag where he and Madzizi had sent their offerings on their way. When Ctarl saw who was waiting, his foot slipped, and he crashed heavily to the ground at his father's feet.

"You," Rtean growled, bending over him. "After all this time—thought you were dead, I did!"

Ctarl couldn't find words. If he'd been standing, maybe; he'd grown immensely since Tinaamy took him in, and might even be his father's equal in height by now. But sprawled on the ground, it felt like he was a child still and Rtean had knocked him down again. Like nothing whatsoever had changed.

Madzizi intervened when Rtean tried to grab him by the shoulders—to lift him up or shake him, Ctarl didn't know which. She broke the half-formed grip with a vicious twist. "Don't you *dare* touch the Prophet of Driftwood."

"Prophet!" Rtean laughed nastily. "So it's true. You ran away to start scamming people with some story about a god saving you. All my effort raising you, and this is what I wind up with: a liar and a cheat."

Only such an insult to his god could have restored Ctarl's tongue, and his spine. "It isn't a scam," he stammered, rising and motioning for Madzizi to back off. "The god found me, and—"

Rtean spat a curse, the only thing he retained from the Mtoek language of his ancestors. "And what? Made you his magic priest? Bollocks. If you're not a cheat, then you're a fool, boy." Then he stepped in closer, his voice lowering to a greasy tone Ctarl remembered all too well. "But a fool who's done well, I hear. Got people feeding you, bringing you all kinds of things. I want a piece of it."

Madzizi had given them just enough distance not to hear that part. Ctarl felt hot and cold all over. Fear and disgust warred within him, just like they used to when he was a boy—when he'd run into the Crush to get away from this man.

That memory was his shield. "If you want to join the faithful," Ctarl said, his voice steadying, "then you are welcome to submit yourself to the initiation. Enter the Crush, give yourself over to the god of Driftwood, and be returned to us; then you and I will talk."

He finished even though Madzizi was frantically signaling him not to. What better answer could there be? Roughly one in ten never returned; the god in the Crush had intervened to save Ctarl from this very man. The odds that Rtean would come back were low.

The odds that Rtean would agree were even lower.

But to his shock, his father only laughed and clapped him on the shoulder. "Sure, boy. Whatever you say."

It was either the first miracle Ctarl had performed, or else his father was planning something. Either way, he needed time to think. "Tonight," he said. "Just before the sun here sets. I'll bless you and send you on your way."

Rtean cocked his gaze at the sky, calculating. "Sun here goes at a steady pace? More than enough time for a drink, then. You wouldn't begrudge your father a thing like that, would you, before doing something so dangerous?"

He wasn't inviting Ctarl to join him. Ctarl dug in his pocket and came up with two of the small nuts a few local bars would accept as currency, then shoved them into his father's hand. Whistling, the man sauntered off.

Watching him go, Madzizi said, "I didn't know your father was a one-blood."

Was that doubt in her voice? Ctarl said firmly, "My mother was a Drifter, through and through. And my father may be full-blooded Mtoe, but he's lived in the Shreds his whole life, and so have I. If he's even still got a world somewhere, I don't know where it is." Maybe one of the uninhabitable ones. Or maybe it was already in the Crush, being slowly ground out of existence. For all Ctarl knew, it was that patch of sea he'd fallen into years ago.

Either his words reassured her, or her other worries were bigger. "Do you want us with you tonight?"

Ctarl normally conducted the initiations alone. Right now, he was grateful for that tradition. "No. I'll deal with him myself." That way there would be no one to see if his father reduced him to the cowering boy he'd once been.

But I'm not a boy. He was a priest, the leader of his flock. And he was going to make his father see that.

The crag cast a long shadow. It was only because Ctarl knew his father's habits that he was able to pick out the second shadow inside it, Rtean sitting with his back against the stone, sipping from a hollowed-out gourd. Filled, no doubt, with something potent.

If his father wanted to go into the Crush drunk, so be it. "Are you ready?" Ctarl asked.

Rtean sniffed and spat to one side, as if to clear his mouth. "Ready to talk, sure. This cult you've got going—"

"It isn't a cult," Ctarl said hotly.

His eyes were adjusting enough to see his father inside the deep shadow, and to see the man's lip curl. "You're leading your own made-up religion, boy, and you've got sheep giving you what they earn. I've been in Driftwood long enough to know a cult when I see one."

The point wasn't worth arguing—any of the points, that they shared what they had, that his followers were his friends, that Ctarl and Madzizi might have invented the rituals but the religion itself was real. They could discuss that when—if—his father came out of the Crush. "Are you ready?"

Rtean levered himself to his feet. His balance was unsteady, but Ctarl knew better than to think that made him any less dangerous. "I'm not going into the Crush."

"Then you have no place here."

His father's breath reeked of the fermented milk sold in Vep, the nearest Shred with any inhabitants. "Oh, I'll pretend. Head a bit in that direction, hide myself behind something—is that what you did? Lucky so many of your sycophants have survived, if they're all running in there thinking they're copying you. Probably most of them do exactly what I'm going to."

"The faithful," Ctarl said coldly, "have been saved by their god. And if He chooses to save you as well, I'll accept His decision. But you have only two choices tonight: go into the Crush for real and take your chances with the god of Driftwood, or go home."

"Home?" Rtean's laugh was a bitter thing, chased with another swig of milk. "It's gone. And the one after that, too, and the one after *that*. No, I'm staying here. And that's only the start, boy, because I'm not going to play rat to your piper. You'll come up with some good story for me, some sign of how your made-up god favors me above the rest of them—oh, don't worry; I'm not going to try to take over your cult. I don't want the work of running the thing, getting up every day to pray and throw things off that rock. But lots of religions have important father figures. I want to be one of them."

Before Ctarl could say anything, Rtean's hand

shot out and seized him by the front of his shirt. "And don't *think* about setting your sheep on me, boy. I didn't come here without some way of defending myself." His free hand patted one pocket. "You try to throw me out, a lot more than one in ten of your followers is going to die."

Ctarl's mouth was as dry as dust. The old habits of terror warred with the strength he'd found since he went into the Crush. Living with his father, he'd never thought past surviving the day, the hour, every heartbeat of Rtean's frequent rages. But when he spoke to his faithful, when he conducted the ceremonies atop the crag's peak . . . then he found a measure of peace.

Now it gave him his voice. "I understand. Come with me."

Rtean made a suspicious sound when Ctarl began to climb the rock. Ctarl paused long enough to say, "This has become a holy site for us—the only place you can look *down* into the Crush. It will be more believable to everyone else if you and I start there."

If a part of him had been hoping Rtean would slip, fall, and break his leg, that part was disappointed. Despite the drink in him, Rtean made it to the top without any injury worse than a few scraped knuckles. He celebrated by draining his gourd, then flinging it in the general direction of the Crush. "There you go. My first offering to your made-up god."

The continual disbelief stung. Ctarl had faced it from many people, but despite everything, down in the bedrock of his soul, he still wanted his father's approval. He always would—and he would never be satisfied.

Like the Crush itself, and the stories others told about the eternal hunger of the god there.

Ctarl pointed into the massed fragments that lay beyond the inner edge of the inhabited Shreds. "That's where it happened."

"Sure, whatever." His father pressed one hand to his stomach as if the milk was disagreeing with him.

"You need to know the story," Ctarl said. "Because you see, Father—I didn't run away to start a scam, or a cult, or even a new religion. I ran to get away from *you*."

His voice grew stronger as he went on, even as his father turned to stare at him. "I was trying to die," Ctarl said. "That's how bad life with you was: I decided I'd rather be torn apart in the Crush than live another moment with you. The god of Driftwood saved me from death, but He also saved me from *you*."

Rtean laughed and spread his arms. "Then your god is as powerless and false as I already thought. Here I am, boy! You're not free of me, and you never will be. I just want what I deserve, after all these years. After everything Driftwood has taken from me."

"Driftwood has taken from us all," Ctarl said. A strange serenity was coming over him, not unlike what he'd felt when the god rescued him. "Together we endure . . . but separately we die."

One way or another, his father was going into the Crush.

He didn't stop to wonder what weapon Rtean had in his pocket. The old man was so used to cowing his son into servile desperation, it never occurred to him that Ctarl didn't need his flock to defend himself.

Three steps was all it took. Three steps and a shove, and his father was gone, over the edge of the rock to the ground far, far below.

After a few, shaking breaths, Ctarl steadied enough to look over the edge.

The shadows down there were even deeper, full night in whatever nameless fragment of a Shred Rtean had fallen into. But he could make out the second shadow within the first, sprawled at unnatural angles and unmoving.

"It's all right, Father," Ctarl said. "Ends are good. They hurt, but then they stop."

That was when the miracle happened:

Even as Ctarl was watching, his father's body disappeared.

He'd made an offering in blood, and the Crush had accepted.

The god of Driftwood was pleased with His priest.

Ctarl wasn't sure how he made it down from the rock, unless it was his god guiding his steps. At the base he walked a few unsteady steps, then halted, staring. Torn between horror and exaltation.

He wasn't the first to believe in a god of Driftwood. Ctarl was just the first to see that god as a savior, rather than an eternally hungry maw. As something to be thanked rather than fed. But now . . .

Rtean's body vanishing. Not even his boots left behind.

Our god is the god of Drifters, not of one-bloods.

The movement got far too close before Ctarl noticed and looked up, but it was only Madzizi. Her bronzed face looked pale in the darkness. "First of Us—"

The formal address steadied him. "My Second," Ctarl breathed, reaching out for her. "A revelation has come to me. The god of Driftwood has spoken."

She caught his hands in her own. "I was watching, First of Us. In case something happened, in case you needed my help. I saw—your father—"

Her eyes were good in the dark, much better than Ctarl's. *I saw you push him off the peak.*

"An offering," Ctarl said. "As we've given before . . . but this time, oh, Madzizi, this time was different." The body disappearing before his eyes, leaving only a stain of blood at the base of the peak. A living offering—but the god of Drifters would not want Drifter blood shed in His name.

It was one-bloods that He hungered for.

Ctarl's grip shifted, clasping Madzizi's hands between his palms. "This is what He wants, my Second. What He has *always* wanted. We Drifters—we've always thought of ourselves as the ones who live in the gaps, with no world of our own. And we've thought we are lesser because of it. But don't you see? Driftwood *is* our world. It belongs to *us*, not to them, not to the one-bloods."

He smiled at Madzizi, the light of revelation suffusing him. "This is why the god spared all of us from the Crush. So that we can make Driftwood the world, the *home*, that it should be."

Madzizi's hands slipped from between his. "Ctarl—First of Us—*no*."

"Yes!" he insisted. "My father's body vanished, Madzizi! Just as things vanish when the Crush takes them. The offering was accepted."

"We aren't that close to the Crush," she said. "Things here don't vanish that fast, Ctarl. And—"

The anguish that strangled her voice dimmed his inner light for a moment. "What is it?"

She walked away from him, going to the towering

rock and pressing her fists against it, head bowed. He thought for a moment that she might be praying. But then she spoke, without lifting her head, her voice dead with despair. "You're the only one our god has ever saved."

It made no sense. "I saw you walk into the Crush, and come out again. You told me—"

"I lied."

Those two words silenced Ctarl as effectively as his father's fist had ever done.

Madzizi punched the rock once, not pulling the blow. "I went just far enough that you couldn't see me, and then I hid and waited. And everybody who's come after, I told them to do the same thing. Oh, I dressed it up in much fancier terms; I said they should meditate on death, on their own dissolution, that they should go into the Crush in their hearts, in their *minds*. But not with their bodies."

The face she turned to him was sick with pain she'd been hiding since the beginning. "The ones who died . . . I assume they didn't listen to me. Or they just got unlucky, and they were the thing that happened to vanish, even though they didn't go too close. But I think most of them didn't listen."

One in ten dead—but nine in ten, he thought, had been saved.

Except his father had been right all along. Ctarl was running a scam. What he thought he'd built was a lie, and his faithful were liars in turn—

"*You* are chosen," Madzizi whispered. "The rest of us . . . I was afraid we wouldn't be."

Ctarl's heart was beating too fast. It felt like the weight of the Crush was on him again, pressing all the air from his lungs. *You are chosen.* That part wasn't a lie. And his followers, they believed; it wasn't their fault what Madzizi had told them wasn't what he'd intended. Maybe it was better that way, so he didn't have a litany of Unokucatuins to haunt his remaining days.

But he couldn't deny what he'd seen tonight. The god of Driftwood had shown Ctarl what He wanted.

"You *are* chosen," Ctarl said. "By me. Chosen to help me make this place what it should be. We'll cleanse the Shreds first, and show our fellow Drifters the truth of our way; then, once they're on our side, we'll take our faith outward. To the Ring, to the Edge, to the Mist itself, until all of Driftwood is ours."

Madzizi's guilt withered in the fire of something new: horror. "You can't mean . . . war against the onebloods?"

"Not at first," Ctarl said. "We don't have the strength for that. But in time, if it is necessary—if that is what our god calls for—then yes."

She backed a step away, then another. She'd lost track of where she was standing: her back ran up against the rock where they'd performed their rituals together for so long. "Ctarl, no! I wanted us to have some purpose, something other than making offerings and supporting each other—but not *this*."

"I didn't choose it, my Second. This is faith: when my god shows me a sign, I must listen."

"And become a murderer?!"

The word flew like a knife for Ctarl's heart. But it met with the shield and armor of his faith.

"It is not murder," Ctarl said. "It is sacrifice."

Madzizi shook her head, mouth twisting in revulsion. "Then I am your Second no more. And you, Ctarl, are no prophet."

She did what damage she could, spreading the truth of what she'd done with the initiates. Some of them abandoned Ctarl. Others claimed they hadn't listened to her misguided advice; they'd gone deep into the Crush and experienced the same salvation Ctarl had. He doubted them, but he didn't mind, because the initiations didn't matter anymore. He declared all those who had stayed were in the chief rank of his followers, and those who came after had to submit to their lead.

Because others came hard on their heels. It was as Ctarl had suspected: more than a few Drifters were ready for the message he brought. Not enough for a war, but plenty for a strategic selection of offerings, bringing him one-bloods to sacrifice to the Crush.

They started in Vep, which had only two, and only one of those native to Vep itself; Ctarl rationed them out slowly, and in the meanwhile his flock took that Shred as their new base of operations.

It was the right place, he felt. Vep was the closest inhabited patch surrounding the Crush; few people even wanted to go so near, let alone live there. And no one would be eager to attack it. Drifters might proclaim their defiance by maintaining the series of bars known as Spit in the Crush's Eye, but they were as superstitious as anyone, and didn't like to go near the place where everything ended. Ctarl and his people had no fear, and that kept them safe.

A series of sacrifices, beginning with his father. None of the others vanished the way Rtean had when Ctarl threw them off the peak, but that was all right. He couldn't expect a miracle every time.

One came to him anyway.

How the man got into Ctarl's bedroom, Ctarl didn't know. He no longer slept in the same room as his followers; they insisted on him taking the chamber that had belonged to the one native-born Vepa. It wasn't sumptuous, but it was as good as they were going to manage this close to the Crush.

Some of his newer followers had been talking about putting a guard on Ctarl's chambers, but he'd dissuaded them, saying the lock on the door was enough. Now he regretted that. Because the man who was waiting for him was clearly a one-blood.

There was no mistaking it. Silver-blue skin, black eyes and hair and nails, and the cold expression of someone who utterly condemned what Ctarl and his people were doing.

"I should never have saved you."

The shout rising in Ctarl's throat died unvoiced. "What?"

"Back when you ran into the Crush. I saw you go by—not the first I've seen go there to commit suicide, but you looked like you were just a kid. You *were* just a kid. So I followed you and dragged you out. Took you to Tinaamy and paid for your healing. I was in a generous mood that day." His lips flattened. "Apparently that was a mistake."

"You're lying," Ctarl said, out of pure reflex. "Tinaamy found me inside their locked house—"

The man held up something that looked like a key made of glass. "You mean, like you just found me inside your locked room?"

Before Ctarl could respond, he went on, remorselessly. "Tinaamy knew. I came back a while later to see if you'd survived, and they told me you'd decided some god in the Crush had saved you. Seemed harmless enough, and I didn't want you coming after me in your gratitude, so I told them to let you go on thinking that. But what you're doing now . . . Tinaamy came to find me themself. The way they figure it, I'm the only one who can convince you to stop."

It *should* have been a lie. A transparent bid to convince him to spare the one-bloods—except if someone wanted to do that, they would have sent a Drifter. Ctarl would have been more willing to believe one of his own people.

A Drifter, though, wouldn't have had a voice he remembered through the haze of pain and approaching death. A voice that had said, *Come on. You'll be all right.*

"You're not the first to get this idea, you know," the man went on, pocketing the glass key. "Either that Driftwood has a god, or that what Drifters should be doing is slaughtering all the one-bloods. Just like sometimes the one-bloods decide the way to save their world is to kill everybody who doesn't belong to it. Nobody succeeds, but a lot of people die along the way, and it doesn't change a fucking thing in this place. Worlds still end. The Crush still wins. All you do is help it happen faster."

Ctarl's legs wouldn't hold him. He managed to stagger to his narrow bed, with the mangy velvet covering he always refused to use and his new Second kept putting back in place. It was unpleasantly soft beneath him as he sank down. "But—everyone who goes into the Crush dies. Except for me. Except for you."

An impatient sigh answered him. "You weren't in

the Crush. I mean, not that there are clear boundaries—but what was killing you was the wall that collapsed on you when you stumbled into it."

That oppressive weight, crushing all the breath from him. "Nobody goes in there," Ctarl said. His eyes burned; he hadn't been blinking. "But you were there."

"Who says nobody goes in there? People hide out in the fringes sometimes, because they know they'll be uninhabited, and nearly everybody is too afraid to chase them. I take bounties to track those people down and drag them back to whoever wants justice."

Ctarl's mind felt like the jumble of fragments in the Crush, except that instead of disintegrating, they were realigning themselves into new, better positions. Making a structure that was whole and strong. This man took bounties to chase people who went to the Crush, despite the risk; he'd braved that risk to save Ctarl, as if it didn't frighten him in the least. He talked about Driftwood's past like he'd seen it.

There were stories. Children's tales, Ctarl had thought. Impossibilities. That sooner or later Driftwood encompassed everything within its sphere, and one of those things was a true immortal: a man who had outlived his lifetime and his world alike.

"You're Last," he whispered.

"Yes. Now, are you going to call off your crusade,

or am I going to have to find another way to stop you?"

"But my father's body disappeared," Ctarl said, still disjointed. "I watched it vanish. It was a miracle—"

Last had a whole repertoire of impatient sounds, it seemed, each one more aggravated than the last. "It was Mtoek. That happens when they die; their bodies vanish. Who knows whether yours will, half Mtoek and all. I'd rather not find out now, unless you force me to. Make up whatever story you like for your followers; it seems like you're pretty good at those. You even convince yourself. Do that now, or—"

He stopped, because Ctarl had slid off the bed and onto his knees. Then Ctarl pressed his forehead to the floor. "I don't have to make anything up. This time—truly—this time, I understand."

Suspicion layered over the impatience. "Understand what?"

"That You," Ctarl said, "are the god of Driftwood."

Silence. Ctarl could feel the beating of his heart—but this time it was a steady, even rhythm. Not the panicked delusions of before. He was right that the god of Driftwood had saved him. He'd just misunderstood everything about what that meant.

"No," Last said, flat and crisp. "I'm not."

"How else do you explain Your immortality? The fact that even the Crush won't touch You?"

"I can't. It doesn't matter. I'm not a god. I just came here to tell you to stop murdering people—"

"At once," Ctarl said, and rose up just enough to bow again. The wood of the floorboards printed itself on his forehead; he would have pressed his face right through them if he could. "I have sinned. I have murdered the innocent in Your name; I have risked the lives of my followers, believing that You would intervene to save them. Some died because of it." The relief of true revelation was mixing with hideous guilt, tearing his voice ragged. "Set whatever penance for me that You wish, or even insist on my life in recompense; it is Yours. I—"

Last jerked him to his feet. "*I'm not a god.* I'm a man who dragged you out from under a broken wall too far from the true heart of the Crush for either of us to be in real danger from it. I don't want you worshipping me; I just want you to stop this idiotic cult business of yours and let people get back to whatever lives they can manage in this cosmic joke we call Driftwood."

"Their lives," Ctarl said. "Yes. That is Your first tenet, then—that people should be free to live their lives, Drifter and one-blood alike."

"Yes—damn it, *no!* Yes to the idea, but no to the tenet." Last let go of him and raked his dark-nailed hands through his hair. "What will it take to make you let go of this nonsense?"

Despite everything, the horror and the guilt and

the mistakes, Ctarl smiled at his god. "You may test my faith if You wish. I deserve whatever trials You choose to set for me. But I will never forsake You."

He did everything Last told him to, except that one thing.

He gave his people a story to turn them away from targeting one-bloods. It just happened that the story he gave them was true: that the god of Driftwood had come to him again, in person, and explained the magnitude of Ctarl's misunderstanding and crimes.

Not all of them believed him. A few—the blood-thirsty core of his new followers, who had come to him when he began the sacrifices—tried to continue without him. Ctarl wrestled with his new faith, debating whether it was right to leave them alone, or right to take action so that others could live their lives in safety. Then he remembered that Last had been willing to kill *him* to stop the murders; from that he could take guidance.

Ctarl's own hands were too stained already, though. It was a few of his true faithful, the ones who stayed even after the new revelation, who took care of it.

Afterwards, though, he disbanded even those. Last had told him to stop the "cult business," so Ctarl could not be a leader any longer. It took a great deal of arguing, and in the end he moved across the Shreds to get away from those who would not give up.

But he didn't abandon his faith.

And neither did others.

A rumor came to him some time later, when Ctarl was sick with a bloody cough and suspected he wouldn't live much longer. A new cult—or rather an old one, under new leadership. Madzizi had heard the stories, and picked up the torch Ctarl had laid down.

Except that her faith was different. It wasn't about war, or killing, or sacrifice. It was about preservation. Last endured; therefore, it was the duty of His followers to preserve what they could. Beginning, she said, with the stories about His deeds.

"Good," Ctarl whispered when he heard. She'd been the wiser one from the start. She'd known that what Ctarl was doing was wrong . . . but the spark at the heart of it was true.

It meant he could face the end with a calm soul. Driftwood and its god were in good hands. And whatever waited for Ctarl on the other side, he trusted Last would see him through.

recorded by Yilime

The Community

OME OF THE AUDIENCE try to leave at the beginning of Teryx's story. They've had dealings with one branch or another of the cult before; they don't want to sit through more proselytization.

But the blue-robed believers are still standing in front of the sole archway that leads from the amphitheater, and they aren't letting anyone through. Not even as Teryx's story draws to a close, as dawn draws near. One winged attendee takes flight from the top of the stands, but the rest stay until she's done.

"You worship Last?" Noirin says in disbelief when Teryx stops talking. "I've seen his memories. He isn't lying to you all out of false modesty or some desire to trick you. He truly isn't a god."

Teryx reaches for Noirin's face as if to stroke her

cheek, and only smiles again—that same peaceful, beatific smile—when Noirin knocks her hand away. "Yes, you carry some of His memories. I heard that He'd been seen dancing in Quinendeniua. Such a blessing for you! Truly, He has honored you above others."

"A blessing she paid him for," Kuondae mutters from the benches. She casts an uneasy glance at the sky.

Noirin leans forward, searching Teryx's eyes as if she can find the truth in their depths. One hand rises to her mouth—and Febrenew almost knocks one of his bottles to the ground. A lot of business gets done at Spit in the Crush's Eye, and he only hears about half of it . . . but this is part of that half.

Noirin bites down on the nut she's palmed into her mouth, cracking its shell, and breathes the dust it contains into Teryx's face.

The cult leader recoils, coughing. Febrenew grins and sets the wine bottle back in place. Not everything works on everybody, but he has yet to hear of anyone who's immune to this. He's only surprised there are still any truthnuts for sale in Driftwood.

"Tell me," Noirin says, her voice cold. "Did you truly see Last walk into the Crush?"

The dust from the heart of a truthnut doesn't compel anyone to speak; it only prevents them from lying. But Teryx, once she stops coughing, doesn't flinch from answering. "He sat for a long time on the stump of the tree in Latch, looking into the Crush. He knew I was watching Him—"

Noirin is no fool, and she's clearly aware of the limitations of the dust. "Do you have proof that he knew, or do you only think it?"

"I think it," Teryx admits. "But even those who believe He is only a man would agree that He is alert to his surroundings. It is very unlikely that He did not notice me."

That's enough to satisfy Noirin. "Go on."

"I said my prayers quietly," Teryx says, "because I know that He does not wish to be disturbed by our worship. Then He closed his eyes. I do not think He was troubled; His look was, to me, one of peace. When He opened his eyes, He looked at something in his hand and sighed."

"What was it?"

"I could not see."

Small enough to fit into Last's palm . . . there are countless things that could be, ranging from the ordinary to the sentimental to the magical. Teryx says, "He stood and slipped whatever it was into His pocket. Then he walked out of Latch, across the rubble of Alok Rath, and through the rain of a world whose name we have unfortunately lost."

"And then?"

The entire amphitheater seems to be holding its breath, waiting for the answer. Teryx knows it, too. She walks away from Noirin, toward the front of the stage, and turns her radiant expression on the assembled crowd. "And then the light flared and I felt in my bones a strange harmony, as if the very substance of Driftwood itself sang. Overcome, I fell to my knees, and when my vision cleared Last was gone.

"He has transcended!" Teryx's voice rings throughout the amphitheater. "The god of Driftwood has accepted His divinity at last! No longer bound by flesh, He has become one with his realm, and is with us all now. Give thanks to your god, and praise His name!"

Even without the dust of a truthnut working on her, no one could doubt Teryx's belief in her words. It echoes back in the voices of her followers, crying out, "Praise His name!"

Their proclamation seems to shake the ground itself. Then the shaking grows stronger, and it becomes obvious to everyone the cultists have nothing to do with it.

"Earthquake!" shouts one of the Drifters, a woman who knows them well from her work out on the Edge.

But few people there know what to do in an earthquake. They crouch helplessly where they are, or try to move and get tossed from their feet. Febrenew goes under his table, while around him all the bottles and cups crash down to shatter on the stone.

A deeper crashing comes from a little distance away, and with it, a cut-off scream. Only when the shaking subsides do people raise their heads and see what has happened.

The archway that leads to the amphitheater floor has collapsed. A foot and the hem of a silver-blue robe are all that can be seen of the cultist who didn't leap clear in time. The rest are helping each other back to their feet, exchanging frightened glances and whispers.

All but Teryx. She kneels before the pile of memorial tokens, hands raised to the sky. "He has shown us His will! We have come here to honor Him, and here we shall stay!" Her wild laughter seems to light the amphitheater itself.

But the light isn't coming from Teryx.

Febrenew lurches over the sea of shattered crockery. "I don't give a piss in the Crush what you believe. Dawn's coming. We have to get out of here, *now*."

Eshap and several other Drifters are already digging at the rubble, trying to see if they can clear a passage. Others didn't realize the problem until Febrenew gave it voice, and now they shriek in sudden fear.

One of the cultists tries to stop Eshap. Then he doubles over, because Dreceyl has cannoned headfirst into his stomach. Noirin cries out, "God or no god, you know Last doesn't want people being killed in his name!"

She inhaled some of the dust herself when she spat it in Teryx's face, but it doesn't take magic to make her words true. Lazr-iminya begins organizing the Drifters working at the archway, while Ioi runs to the top of the amphitheater and begins to shout, waving her arms. Not many of the people present for the memorial can fly, but those who can grab the smallest of the trapped—Febrenew's lizard-like cup-washer; the squirming and protesting Dreceyl—and carry them out. If the fliers lurch to the ground with more speed and less grace than usual, that's still better than remaining where they are.

One of them comes back, bearing the top end of a ladder, followed by some ropes. Soggeny lies on the other side of that wall, and the people there are doing what they can. Down at the archway, a tiny gap opens, and Kuondae is the first to wiggle through it, while others curse her for saving her own furry hide. But not long after she vanishes, two of the rock-munchers from Skyless show up and begin chewing their way through the collapsed stone from the other end. They avoid this place when they can, which means someone must have sent them.

Even the cultists help. The scribe's hands bleed as he tears at the rubble blocking their way. Whatever Teryx may say, they didn't come to the amphitheater to die.

But Teryx herself stays, kneeling in front of the memorial, hands spread and face turned to the sky. The final Drifter out through the collapsed tunnel hears her laughing.

Then no one hears anything at all. And when one of the fliers glides by to take a look, carefully keeping to the safe air above Soggeny, all he sees is the empty floor of the amphitheater, and the pile of gifts laid there in Last's name.

Safely in the subterranean chambers of Skyless, Noirin kicks one foot out in frustration. "I waited too long. And I didn't expect a *cult*."

"They've been around for ages," Febrenew says. "Longer than probably anything except Last himself. He told me they come and go, sort of—different groups, different spins on the idea of his divinity. More of them at some times than others. A lot of them, lately." That might be why Last thought about forgetting.

On the far side of the chamber, someone is bandaging the scribe's bleeding hands. His scroll is stuffed through the belt of his robe. Even if Last *had* forgotten, others would remember for him.

"I wanted to question her more," Noirin says, staring at the narrow patch of light that is all that remains of access to the amphitheater. "What she saw . . . where was she standing when it happened? Could Last have simply gone behind something while she wasn't looking? She said it herself, in her story—he goes into the fringes of the Crush sometimes. It doesn't mean he's dead."

Much less transcended. Febrenew shrugs. "Or re-member what Kuondae said. Last does lie, when he needs to. Maybe he staged that on purpose, to make the cultists think he was gone."

"Except that it will only encourage them," Noirin mutters. "They'll spread the word."

Febrenew grimaces. "Yeah. Then again, I'm not sure anything could stop them. Not until Driftwood itself crumbles into dust."

A gust of wind whistles through the crack in the collapsed tunnel, hot and dry. Like the wind in Ioi's story, except not flaying the skin from people's flesh.

Everything exists in Driftwood at some point or another. Like ways to turn people into wind. And in Eshap's story, Qoress took on the appearance of the king, not as an illusion, but for the rest of his life.

Febrenew wonders: is there any way to do that in Driftwood right now?

His map is still in the amphitheater, surrounded by shattered bottles. He doesn't much fancy going back there the next night to retrieve it—and besides, he has two copies ready and waiting. This one can be his own tribute to Last.

Because if the man *has* changed his appearance, then by the time the people of Driftwood notice there's someone else who's been around for far too long to be explained, Febrenew himself will be long gone. If Last is dead, he deserves some kind of me-morial. If he truly is a god—or has become one—

then this can be Febrenew's one and only offering to him.

And if Last shows up later at the new incarnation of Spit in the Crush's Eye, then Febrenew will pour him a drink and they can have a good laugh over this whole affair.

Noirin sighs. "I should get back to Surnyao. I haven't answered my question, not really . . . but my people need me."

"Keep remembering," Febrenew says.

"Keep remembering," she echoes, and walks away.

It has the sound of a blessing.

Smiling at the End of the World

PAGGARAT WAS DOOMED from the start—or rather, from the end. Nothing new about that; every part of Driftwood, every building, every person, every bit of dirt that makes up a world fragment is there because its doom finally came calling, and every last shred of it will eventually fade to nothing. Period, the end, the rest is silence.

But Paggarat was especially doomed. Most worlds are big when they arrive at Driftwood's Edge. They shrink as they go in, of course; time passes, the reality decays, and what was once a country-sized chunk of land with a population big enough to fill cities sitting on the outskirts of this place becomes a three-block ghetto of four inbred families gasping for air in the Crush that is the center of Driftwood. Paggarat was different. Paggarat showed up one day as a farm-sized bit of land with a grand total of two inhabitants.

Bookies in the Shreds put the odds of it surviving for even five of its not particularly long years at a hundred to one.

Thing about the bookies is, they're full of shit. Most of them take your money and vanish to a Shred you never heard of; saves them the hassle of trying to usefully measure time when there are as many suns, moons, seasons, clocks, and calendars as there are dying worlds in Driftwood. More, actually, since some places have several of each. But the bookies really tried to make a go of this one— some did, anyway—because Paggarat was going to be gone so fast they might for once be able to make real wagers on it.

I laughed myself sick over that one, dozens of times in the years and years that Paggarat was in Driftwood. Aun and Esr, they never laughed. They were good people, much better than me. They just smiled at each other and went on living their lives, as the inexorable cycle of Driftwood dragged Paggarat farther and farther in, away from the Edge, through the Shreds (there's a joke; Paggarat was no bigger than a Shred to begin with), and to the lip of the Crush itself.

No idea how they did it. No idea how they kept smiling, kept loving each other, when they were the only survivors of the cataclysm that destroyed their world (except for their farm) and everyone in it (except for themselves). No idea how they could not go crazy when their holy words said two would survive to repopulate their world after the apocalypse, but Esr was barren and there was no world left to repopulate anyway. It wasn't that they believed the new world would come after the Crush ground them out of existence; they said they didn't, and I believed them. I've seen enough people lie about it to know. Driftwood is the end, the end of ends. Nothing comes after that. Only oblivion, and maybe not even that much.

Yet Aun and Esr kept smiling.

Call it madness. Call it denial. Call it whatever; I don't have a word for it. Somehow Aun and Esr smiled through the years as they aged, as Paggarat faded and shrank, as the Crush drew ever closer. Somehow, even though pretty soon there was going to be nothing left of them, of their love, they found peace and contentment in that love, and didn't fear the end. The last time I saw them, Aun was making dinner from the food Esr had begged in the Shreds that day, and she was cleaning the one room they had left.

Then they went into the Crush, and even I wouldn't follow them there.

The only thing that's left of Paggarat is my memory. It was doomed, like the rest of Driftwood, and Aun and Esr with it. It lasted far longer than anyone expected, and so pretty much everybody lost their bets except the lunatics who took the top end, and the bookies wouldn't pay out to them—but that's not why the bettors really lost. Paggarat was less doomed than they wagered, not because of how long it lasted, but because of how it went out.

Because of Aun and Esr, smiling at each other until the end of the world.

MARIE BRENNAN holds an undergraduate degree in archaeology and folklore from Harvard University and pursued graduate studies in cultural anthropology and folklore at Indiana University before leaving to write full-time. Her academic background fed naturally into her work, providing her with the tools to build fantastical worlds.

Her first series, the Doppelganger duology of *Warrior* and *Witch*, came out in 2006. From there she moved to historical fantasy, first with the Onyx Court series: *Midnight Never Come* (2008), *In Ashes Lie* (2009), *A Star Shall Fall* (2010), *With Fate Conspire* (2011), spanning three hundred years of London's history, and then with the acclaimed pseudo-Victorian Memoirs of Lady Trent. The first book of that series, *A Natural History of Dragons* (2013), was a finalist for the World Fantasy Award, and won the Prix Imaginales in France for Best Translated Novel; the final book, *Within the Sanctuary of Wings* (2017), won the RT Reviewers' Choice Award for Best Fantasy Novel. The series as a whole was a finalist for both the Hugo Award and the Grand Prix l'Imaginaire.

Brennan is a member of the Book View Café authors' cooperative, where she has published the Wilders urban fantasies *Lies and Prophecy* (2012) and *Chains and Memory* (2016) as well as several short story collections and nonfiction works, including *Writing Fight Scenes* and the Patreon-supported *New Worlds* series of worldbuilding guides. Her fondness for role-playing games has led her to write both fiction and setting material for several game lines, including *Legend of the Five Rings* and *Tiny d6*. Together with fellow author Alyc Helms, she is the author of the upcoming Rook and Rose epic fantasy trilogy, which will come out under the joint name of M.A. Carrick.

She has taught creative writing to both college students and twelve-year-olds, and run several convention workshops on the art of fight scenes. When not writing or playing RPGs, she practices photography and shōrin-ryū karate. She lives with her husband in the San Francisco Bay Area.